THE FACE IN THE BESSLEDORF FUNERAL PARLOR

Books by
PHYLLIS REYNOLDS NAYLOR

THE WITCH TRILOGY

Witch's Sister
Witch Water
The Witch Herself

Walking through the Dark

AUTOBIOGRAPHY

How I Came to Be a Writer

How Lazy Can You Get?
Eddie, Incorporated

THE YORK TRILOGY

Shadows on the Wall
Faces in the Water
Footprints at the Window

All Because I'm Older

The Boy with the Helium Head
A String of Chances
The Solomon System

Night Cry
Old Sadie and the Christmas Bear
The Dark of the Tunnel
The Keeper
The Year of the Gopher
Beetles, Lightly Toasted
Maudie in the Middle
One of the Third-Grade Thonkers
Keeping a Christmas Secret
Send No Blessings
King of the Playground
Shiloh

THE BESSLEDORF BOOKS

The Mad Gasser of Bessledorf Street
The Bodies in the Bessledorf Hotel
Bernie and the Bessledorf Ghost
The Face in the Bessledorf Funeral Parlor

THE ALICE McKINLEY BOOKS

The Agony of Alice
Alice in Rapture, Sort Of
Reluctantly Alice
All but Alice
Alice in April

Josie's Troubles
The Grand Escape

THE FACE IN THE BESSLEDORF FUNERAL PARLOR

Phyllis Reynolds Naylor

A Jean Karl Book

ATHENEUM 1993 NEW YORK
Maxwell Macmillan Canada
Toronto
Maxwell Macmillan International
New York Oxford Singapore Sydney

Atheneum
Macmillan Publishing Company
866 Third Avenue
New York, NY 10022

Maxwell Macmillan Canada, Inc.
1200 Eglinton Avenue East
Suite 200
Don Mills, Ontario M3C 3N1

Macmillan Publishing Company is part of the Maxwell Communication Group of Companies.

First edition
Printed in the United States of America
10   9   8   7   6   5   4   3   2   1

Library of Congress Cataloging-in-Publication Data
Naylor, Phyllis Reynolds.
The face in the Bessledorf Funeral Parlor / Phyllis Naylor. —1st ed.
p.   cm.
"A Jean Karl book."
Summary: Convinced that the strange things happening at the funeral parlor next door to his family's hotel are somehow connected to a recent robbery, Bernie determines to become famous by proving his theory and catching the thief.
ISBN 0–689–31802–2
[1. Mystery and detective stories.] I. Title.
PZ7.N24Fab 1993
[Fic]—dc20   92–32613

TO PAT SCALES,
WHO KNOWS WHERE TO FIND A GOOD STORY

CONTENTS

THE FACE IN THE BESSLEDORF FUNERAL PARLOR

One

COME AS YOU ARE

The Bessledorf Hotel was at 600 Bessledorf Street, between the bus depot and the funeral parlor. Officer Feeney said that some folks came into town on one side of the hotel and exited on the other. The Bessledorf had thirty rooms, not counting the apartment where Bernie Magruder's family lived, and Feeney said that a robber, a liar, or a cheat could be in any one of them.

"How do you know?" asked eleven-year-old Bernie.

"'Cause there are lots of 'em around, and they've got to be somewhere," the policeman said.

"I'll bet I'd know if we had a robber staying in our hotel," Bernie told him.

"Bet you wouldn't. Robbers look just about like everyone else. *Better'n* most folks, actually, because they've got what the regular folks are missing."

At lunch, in the apartment behind the registration

1

desk, Bernie told his family what Officer Feeney had said.

"Feeney has bananas where his brains should be," said Delores, Bernie's sister, who was twenty years old and the eldest of the four Magruder children. "*Every*body, according to Feeney, is a suspect, and I can only say that I might marry a stuntman, a sky diver, or a human cannonball, but I would never, ever, marry a policeman."

"Ha!" said Joseph, the next oldest. "Delores is so picky she'll probably not marry at all. Officer Feeney sees criminals wherever he looks because that's what he's paid to do."

"Well, *I'm* paid to sew straps and pound grommets at the parachute factory, but I don't go around seeing parachutes that aren't there!" Delores declared.

"My dear, dear family," said Mr. Magruder from one end of the table. "Why are we arguing? Why are we disturbed? Life has never been better for the Magruders. We live in a magnificent old hotel in a lovely old town, and it is due to the hard work and tenacity of the Magruder family that the hotel is what it is today."

"Leaking?" said Bernie.

"Well, leak it might, in a place or two, but it is the finest hotel in Middleburg, and I'm proud to be the manager."

"It is the *only* hotel in Middleburg," said his

2

wife, "but we intend to keep it that way. As long as our rooms are clean, our prices low, and our food good, there will never be a reason for another hotel to open here."

"Unless we have robbers," whispered Lester.

Everyone turned to look at Bernie's younger brother, who was nine, making ketchup soup in a cereal bowl. To a cup of red ketchup he had added some water, his peas, his pork chop, and half a potato. Bernie couldn't watch.

"Robbers?" said his mother.

"Yes," said Lester. "I left a candy bar on top of the refrigerator and now it's gone. I'll bet we have robbers already."

"I ate it," said Joseph. "I didn't know it was yours."

"See?" said Lester. "It's just like Feeney said. You can't tell a robber from anyone else."

"We do not have robbers!" Mr. Magruder said, plunking his fork on the table. "We have respectable people in respectable rooms in a respectable hotel in a fine old town, and the *reason* it is a fine old town is because Officer Feeney helps keep it that way. So let's hear no more talk about robbers."

After lunch Bernie went out to sit on the wall by the alley and wait for his friends, Georgene and Weasel. Mixed Blessing, the Great Dane, followed and sat scratching himself in the sunshine. Lewis and Clark, the two cats, walked paw over paw along the top of the wall, and it was only when the cement truck, parked behind the funeral parlor, started up again, that the cats skittered behind the garbage cans.

Weasel, whose glasses slid continually down his nose, soon came up the alley, Georgene Riley behind him on her skateboard, ponytail flying.

"What's happening at the funeral parlor?" Georgene asked.

"I don't know," Bernie said. "Last week they built a bay window. Now they're redoing their driveway."

"There's hardly room for a driveway between the funeral parlor and the hotel as it is," said Georgene. She crawled up on the wall beside Bernie. "What do you suppose it's like to live in a funeral home? I mean, do you think everyone wears black suits to the table?"

"They eat blackberries for breakfast, black bean soup for lunch, and black bread for dinner," said Weasel, grinning.

Georgene giggled. "They have black sheets on their beds and wear black pajamas."

"And they beat their children black and blue," said Weasel.

Bernie laughed. "Naw. They're not like that at all. Moe and Joe wear baseball caps when they're not on duty, and Woe has been there forever, Dad said."

"Woe?"

"He's the father. Woe, Moe, and Joe. The funeral

home used to be called Woe and Sons, but they changed it to the Bessledorf Funeral Parlor."

"But do they ever smile?" asked Georgene. "They always seem so serious."

"They're just like anyone else," said Bernie. "If bodies are going to be embalmed and buried, *somebody* has to do it. It's a job. That's what Dad says, anyway."

He couldn't understand, therefore, when he went inside later, why his parents were so upset with the men at the funeral parlor.

"The most tasteless thing I can think of!" said Bernie's mother.

"They never even asked my opinion," said Theodore, Bernie's dad.

"People will be driving through here at all hours of the night!" complained Delores.

"It'll be the laughingstock of Middleburg," said Joseph.

"Ha ha, ha ha," squawked Salt Water, the parrot, shuffling back and forth on his perch.

"Well, *I* can hardly wait!" said Lester, taking a licorice stick that he'd already chewed on out of his pocket. He started to chew it again.

Bernie looked from one member of his family to the other. "What are you talking about?" he asked.

"Go outside and see for yourself," his father told him.

Bernie went to the front door and looked at the funeral parlor again. He expected to see it painted bright pink or something. It looked perfectly all right to him, however. And then he saw the sign on the lawn:

Coming soon!
Bessledorf's First Drive-In Funeral Parlor
No need to dress,
Come as you are.
Pay your respects
From in your car.

Two

ROBBERS, LIARS, AND CHEATS

Bernie tried to figure it out. At a drive-in McDonald's, you ordered a hamburger to go. At a drive-in bank, you got money from a drawer. At a drive-in theater, you watched a movie from your car. What did you get at a drive-in funeral parlor? He was afraid to think.

He was still standing there when Mrs. Buzzwell, Mr. Lamkin, and Felicity Jones came up the walk. They were the "regulars," the three people who, besides the Magruder family, lived in the hotel all year. They, too, saw the sign for the first time.

"Well, I never!" said Mrs. Buzzwell. "What is this world coming to? You wouldn't find *me* lying in a window for all the world to see!"

"That's what they'll do?" asked Bernie, his eyes wide. "Put dead people in the window?"

"Like a loaf of bread or a pair of shoes," said old Mr. Lamkin. "Folks'll drop by to say, 'My, doesn't he look natural!' and go on about their business."

Beside Mrs. Buzzwell, who was large, Felicity Jones looked like a broomstick. She was a thin, young woman who always listed slightly in a strong wind. "It's not good, not good at all!" she said softly. "A spirit likes to know that its body is at rest, and how a body gets any rest with people driving in and out is beyond me."

Just then Officer Feeney came up, and *he* saw the sign.

"Well, if that don't beat all!" he said, scratching his head. "It's not enough that I have to keep my eye on the bus stop, with folks coming and going every which way. Not enough that I have to watch over the Bessledorf Hotel and the parachute factory. Now I've got to check out a body in a drive-in window of a funeral parlor. If this don't make me retire from the force, don't know what will."

Now that he knew what a drive-in funeral parlor was, however, Bernie decided that he didn't much care. He himself didn't plan to be lying in it for a long time yet, and once he was dead, he didn't care whether he was in a window or not.

Bernie didn't worry too much, as a rule, except for three things:

1. He was afraid his dad might lose his job as manager of the Bessledorf Hotel. Mr. Magruder had held a lot of jobs before the family moved to Middleburg, and the Magruder children, Mother always said, had blown about the country like dry leaves in the wind.

Several things had happened in the past to make Bernie think that Dad might lose *this* job. But now business was great, and Mr. Fairchild, the owner of the hotel, who lived in Indianapolis, was pleased. So Bernie hoped that they would stay in Middleburg for a long, long time.

2. Bernie worried that he might never get his name in the *Guinness Book of World Records* as having coasted for the longest distance on a skateboard. He and his friends often went to the top of Bessledorf Hill, up by the parachute factory, to practice. So far he'd rolled only as far as the drugstore on the corner, and he worried that he might never get down as far as the theater.

3. Bernie worried that his sister might not get married and move out. It wasn't that he didn't love Delores, exactly. The trouble was, if she wasn't complaining about one thing, she was complaining about another. Nothing ever seemed to go right for Delores. If she married and moved out, Bernie would probably get her

room. There would be even more space for the animals that Joseph brought home, and animals never complained.

Joseph, who was nineteen and studying to be a veterinarian, said that people always seemed to be leaving unwanted pets tied to the door of the animal clinic. So far he had brought home Mixed Blessing, the Great Dane; Lewis and Clark, the cats; and Salt Water, the parrot. Any more, Mr. Magruder declared, and the hotel would be a zoo. Delores complained the loudest of all. She could never go to the bathroom in the middle of the night, she said, without stepping on a tail or a paw, or hearing a parrot squawk, "Awk! All hands on deck! Awk! Awk!"

Sundays in Middleburg were as quiet as Saturdays were busy. On Saturdays buses pulled into the station more often; more people got out to visit the quaint little shops, tour the courthouse or the parachute factory, or amble down to Middleburg Park, where the Middleburg River flowed on its way to the Wabash.

But on Sundays people quietly went to church in their Sunday best and quietly came to the hotel restaurant for dinner afterward. Bernie's mother always wore her good green dress with the lace collar.

Sunday was also the one day of the week that Mrs. Magruder did not work on her romance novels, which she wrote on the side when things were not too hurried at the desk. *Quivering Lips* had been rejected by seventeen publishers so far, but Bernie's mother said, "Never mind, Rome wasn't built in a day," and started right in on *Shivering Shoulders*.

After the fried chicken dinner at noon, Bernie went out to sit on the wall by the alley again, just as a funeral procession was lining up to leave for the cemetery.

Bernie watched the lineup.

Woe, the father, in his dark blue suit, stood out on the driveway directing the order of the cars. Moe, without his red baseball cap, drove the hearse. Joe, without his yellow cap, drove the car with the deceased's family in it. Moe and Joe were also wearing their dark blue suits.

Bernie always felt sad when the deceased's family went by. Woe, Moe, and Joe always looked sad, too, but then, that was their job.

After the procession left the new driveway and turned onto the street in front of the funeral parlor, Georgene and Weasel came down the alley carrying their skateboards under their arms.

"We didn't think we ought to skate right after a funeral had gone by," Georgene said. "It doesn't seem very respectful of the dead." The three friends sat quietly for a few minutes. But when they felt they had been respectful long enough, they took their skateboards to the top of Bessledorf Hill, and Bernie took the longest running start he had taken yet, then coasted all the way to the bottom, pumping with his arms to make himself go farther. *Clickety, clickety,* went the wheels of his skateboard over the cracks in the sidewalk. *Still* he went no farther than the drugstore. It was very discouraging.

They walked to the bus depot and sat on a bench to wait for a bus to come in.

"Do you know what Feeney said?" Bernie told them. "He said that you couldn't tell a robber, a liar, or a cheat from anyone else—they all look the same."

"I'll bet *I* could," said Georgene.

"Me, too," said Weasel, and when the bus arrived they sat deciding whether each passenger getting off was a robber, a liar, a cheat, or just a normal human being.

Weasel nodded toward a man with a long, thin face.

"Liar," he said.

"Uh-uh." Bernie shook his head. "Normal," he decided.

"No, robber," said Georgene. She watched while a woman in a flowered dress got off.

"Cheat," said Bernie.

"Normal," said Weasel.

And so it went. Nobody could agree.

At dinner that evening Mr. Magruder said, "I hear there will be a grand opening for the drive-in window at the funeral parlor on Thursday. I'm not sure what my duties are regarding this questionable addition to our neighborhood, but I suppose I shall have to attend and look pleased."

"I'm sure you must," said his wife.

"How do they know there will be anyone dead to put in the window?" Lester asked.

"A very good question indeed," said his father.

But Joseph shrugged. "If they've got a body, they show it off. If not, they show the place where it would have been."

"And if the body's cremated, they just put a jar of ashes in the window?" Lester asked.

"If you ask me . . . ," Delores began.

"We didn't," said Bernie.

". . . If you ask me, that drive-in window is the stupidest thing I ever heard of. I might marry an insurance man, an accountant, or a cook, but I could never, ever, marry an undertaker."

Bernie worried more than ever that Delores might never marry at all—that the only way she would ever leave the family would be in a funeral procession of her own.

"Delores," he said, "when you die, do you want to be buried or cremated?"

"Cremated. I want my ashes placed in a little box, tied with a blue ribbon, and sent to Steven Carmichael, who jilted me and broke my heart," Delores said, referring to an old boyfriend. "I would want them strapped to his back and worn for the rest of his natural life so he could never forget me."

"Not I," said Mother. "I don't intend to be cremated. I intend to lie in a mahogany coffin with candles at my head and feet, in my gold velvet gown with the ruffle about the neck. And I want my gravestone to read, 'Here lies the author of *Quivering Lips*, *Shivering Shoulders*, and *Trembling Toes*, who *would* have been a best-selling author if anyone had published her books.'"

"My dear, dear family," said Father. "Why are we talking of death and dying? We are healthy, we have a roof over our heads, and business is wonderful. I'm sorry if all my talk of the drive-in funeral parlor has upset you. We shall attend the ceremony as good neighbors should, and then we shall not say another word about it."

On Monday the coming of Middleburg's first and only drive-in funeral parlor was all but forgotten, because, on the morning news, the radio carried a story of a different sort: "A robbery has been reported at the Higgins Roofing Company. Employees coming to work this morning discovered an empty safe in the blood-stained office of its vice president. Both the retirement fund and the vice president are missing. Police suspect foul play."

Three

MAN IN THE DARK

"What a horrible thing to happen!" Bernie's mother gasped. "Those nice people at Higgins Roofing, thinking their money was safe. Now they've nothing to live on in their old age."

Mr. Magruder was listening to more bulletins on the radio: "The police believe that the vice president was working alone before the office opened, when robbers broke in and a struggle ensued. Police theorize that the vice president was forced to open the safe, after which the robbers took him, dead or alive, with them. An investigation is underway."

Bernie was worried. "Do *you* have a retirement fund, Dad?"

"Why, you children are our retirement fund, Bernie," his father said. "When your mother and I are old, we expect you to take care of us."

"What if something happens to us kids?" asked Lester.

"Then we would be out on the street again, love—blown about the country like leaves in the wind," said Mother.

Bernie worried more than ever.

"Well, if I spent *my* life putting money in a retirement fund and robbers made off with it, I'd go after them myself," Delores declared over her muffin. "Anyone tries to mess with *my* money, he's dead meat, let me tell you."

Bernie believed her.

"The Higgins Company shouldn't have had that money in a safe to begin with," said Joseph, pouring himself some cereal. "If the money had been in a bank where it belonged, it would have been insured."

"Well, no use crying over spilled milk. You can be sure the police are working on it this very minute. If they can find the vice president's body even, they'll get some kind of clue," said Father.

Father was right. The police were working on it. Squad cars drove up and down the street all morning. Georgene and Weasel couldn't even come over. Their parents wanted them to stay home where they would be safe, what with a robber, and possibly even a murderer, on the loose.

Bernie sat around the hotel lobby all day listening

to the drone of the air conditioners and the chatter of guests as they discussed the robbery. When evening came, he took Mixed Blessing for a walk, wandered around the bus station, ate some chocolate cake in the hotel dining room, and finally went into the bedroom he shared with Lester.

He crawled up to the top bunk and stretched out to read some Spiderman comics. He tried not to listen to the constant *crunch, crunch* of Lester eating crackers spread with peanut butter and sprinkled with Cheerios in the bunk below.

"Bernie," said Lester after a minute, "when you die, what are you going to do with your body?"

"I won't do anything, Lester. I'll be dead."

Lester went on crunching his crackers. "If you're embalmed, you're buried in a coffin in one place. But if you have yourself cremated, you can be sprinkled over the whole state of Indiana. Did you know that, Bernie? Over the whole country, even!"

Bernie put his comic book down. "What are you talking about, Lester?"

"It's true. Moe was telling me. He said they cremated a body last week, and the relatives told him just what to do: sprinkle half the remains over the Wabash River and send the rest to Ohio by Federal Express."

Bernie turned out the light. "Go to sleep, Lester."

"After I die," Lester went on, "I want my ashes sprinkled by helicopter."

"Good night, Lester," Bernie told him.

"Over Disneyland," Lester added.

Bernie turned over on his side.

In the dark, Bernie could see out the window. The boys' room faced the narrow driveway between the funeral parlor and the Bessledorf Hotel. His eyes opened and closed, opened and closed. Once, however, when they opened, he thought he saw something crawling up the fire escape on the side of the funeral parlor.

He blinked. He *did* see something! In the dim light of the street lamp, Bernie was sure he saw a man climbing up the side of the building, just behind the new bay window.

"Lester?" he said. "Are you awake?"

Lester grunted.

"I think I just saw Moe or Joe climbing up the fire escape to the roof. The man was wearing the same kind of cap that they wear."

"If it was red, it was Moe. If it was yellow, it's Joe," said Lester.

"It was too dark to tell. Why do you suppose they'd be up on the roof at night?"

"To sprinkle ashes," said Lester. "Float them down on the breeze."

It was a possibility, Bernie had to admit. Morticians probably didn't go around during the day sprinkling ashes where everyone could see. It made sense that

Moe or Joe just might crawl up on the roof at night when there was a good wind, and scatter away. If a body wanted to be scattered, that is. By morning, the ashes would be so scattered that no one would know the difference.

He slipped off his bunk and went to the window. But there was no one on the roof now that he could see. No one at all.

Four

ASHES TO ASHES

"*I saw something strange last night,*" Bernie told Georgene and Weasel the next morning when his friends were finally allowed to come over. "It was either Moe or Joe climbing up to the roof of the funeral parlor, and Lester thinks he was up there to scatter ashes."

"Is *that* what they do with them?" Georgene looked warily about her. "Do you mean that when we sweep the sidewalk, we're actually sweeping up somebody's grandfather?"

"Could be," said Bernie. "Or else the ashes are in the river. Some folks choose a river, Lester says. Maybe they like the thought that after they're gone, they're still sort of floating around."

It was later, when they were cleaning out Salt Water's cage, that Bernie had a thought. An awful thought. An awful, terrible thought.

If, as his father had said, even finding the vice president's body would give the police a clue, it would be smart for the robbers to get rid of it so that it would never be found. And the best way to get rid of a body would be to cremate it and scatter the ashes.

And *if* the robber knew how and where to cremate a body, he would probably be someone who worked in a funeral parlor. Maybe that's what Moe or Joe was doing on the roof last night: scattering the vice president's ashes.

Was it possible? Bernie had to admit that it was. Was it probable? He didn't know Joe or Moe well enough to say, but he surely had never thought of them as robbers, and surely not murderers. He told Georgene and Weasel what he suspected.

"But even if Moe or Joe *was* a robber, how would he know that the vice president had the retirement money in his safe?" Weasel asked.

"Because all the businessmen in Middleburg get together for lunch on Thursdays in our hotel dining room," Bernie said. "They always talk business. Maybe the vice president mentioned that he was looking for a new place to invest the retirement money and was keeping it for a while in his safe. Maybe that's what gave Moe and Joe the idea."

"Moe *and* Joe?" asked Georgene. "Do you think they're both in on it?"

"I don't know which one it was climbing the fire

21

escape, but it would be hard for one to be robbing people and the other not to know about it," Bernie said.

"What would they do with it all?" asked Weasel. "If they put a big chunk of money in the bank all at once, someone might get suspicious. And if they kept it around the house, the police might find it if they searched."

Bernie thought that one over. Then he got a second idea. A second awful, terrible idea. If they wanted to put the money where no one would find it, they would probably bury it along with a corpse or two or three, a little here, a little there. *No* one would look in a grave. Being morticians, though, Woe, Moe, and Joe could go into a cemetery whenever they liked, and nobody would think it unusual.

"They would bury it along with bodies," Bernie answered. "Every time there's a funeral, just after the relatives leave the grave, Moe or Joe could toss in a bag or two of money, fill the grave with dirt, and then come back someday and dig it up."

Georgene shivered. "Are you going to tell Officer Feeney?"

Bernie shook his head. "Not unless I get more proof. If Feeney went over to question them and they *didn't* have anything to do with that robbery, they'd sure be mad at me. They'd make things so unpleasant for us here in Middleburg we might have to move. Dad says that the first rule of staying put is to get along with your neighbors."

Georgene looked around at the street and sidewalk in front of the funeral parlor. "Wouldn't it be awful if the vice president was scattered on the sidewalk this very minute and we were walking right over him?" she said, digging at some dirt that had collected in one corner of the steps.

And Bernie had another idea. "Weasel, why don't you go up to the funeral parlor and ask to talk to Moe or Joe. Tell him you've got two boxes of ashes, one of your aunt and one of your uncle, but you've forgotten which is which. Your aunt wanted to be scattered over California, see, and your uncle wanted to be scattered over New Jersey. You want to know whether experts could tell the difference between a man and woman's remains."

Weasel stared at Bernie, the glasses sliding down farther and farther on his nose until they rested on the very tip. "What good will that do?"

"If he says that experts *can* tell the difference, that means they can tell if it's human ashes at all. We'll collect all the stuff we can find on the steps and sidewalk that looks like ashes, take it to the county coroner, and see if it's the missing vice president."

"You're nuts, Bernie!" said Weasel. "They'll think I'm crazy! It was your idea. *You* do it."

"They might ask which aunt, which uncle. They might even mention it to my folks," Bernie said.

"Well, count me out," Weasel told him.

Georgene got up from the curb where she was sitting and brushed off the seat of her pants. "*I'll* do it," she said.

Bernie and Weasel stared as she opened the big iron gate in front of the funeral parlor, went up the sidewalk, then the steps, and rang the bell.

It was Joe in his yellow baseball cap who answered. Bernie watched as he talked to Georgene. Could he possibly be a robber? A killer and robber both? Could it really have been Joe or his brother who had planned to rob the Higgins Company, kill the vice president, cremate his body, scatter the ashes from the roof of the funeral parlor, and hide the money on top of the next two or three coffins they buried in the cemetery?

"What's she *talking* about so long?" Weasel said nervously, pushing his glasses back up on his nose again and holding them there with one finger. "All she has to do is ask if you can tell men ashes from women ashes."

Bernie was feeling nervous, too. Maybe he *should* have gone himself. "What if they get suspicious, Weasel, and figure Georgene knows?"

"Just keep your eye on Georgene," Weasel told him. "If she goes inside, we go after her. We sure don't want *her* scattered from the roof."

It didn't make sense, though. "Why would any of

them—Moe or Joe or Woe—get involved in a robbery just before they opened Bessledorf's first drive-in funeral parlor?" Bernie said. "They've always been good neighbors. Why would they do something like that now?"

"Maybe it's *because* of that drive-in window," said Weasel. "Maybe they needed the money to pay for redoing the driveway and remodeling the downstairs."

That made sense, too.

Just then the boys saw Georgene come back down the steps of the funeral parlor and out to the curb again.

"What did he say?" Bernie and Weasel asked together.

"He said no, you probably couldn't tell the difference between male and female ashes unless you found a whole tooth in the ashes, and could identify it from the dental records of either my aunt or uncle."

Bernie sighed and looked around. "Even if we *did* find ashes, I wonder if we could tell the difference between fireplace ashes and vice president ashes."

Georgene nodded. "If it's fireplace ashes, you'd find little pieces of bark. If it's human ashes, you'd find little pieces of bone."

Bernie got up off the curb. "Okay, here's what we do. We'll each take a different territory, and sweep up anything that looks like ash around the funeral parlor. We've got to do this before it rains again, or the wind blows the ash far away. If the police don't find the vice president's body soon, we'll turn over the ashes to Officer Feeney and tell him how I saw Joe or Moe climbing up the fire escape after dark, and what we figure they were doing up there."

Bernie and his friends got some empty cereal boxes from the trash cans behind the hotel. Weasel took the alley behind the funeral parlor, Georgene took the driveway between the funeral parlor and the hotel, and Bernie took the sidewalk and steps out front. Whenever Bernie came across a little pile of gray powdery something-or-other, he brushed it carefully up in the palm of one hand and slid it into his box.

Bernie worked a long time. His back and shoulders ached. He used a whisk broom to brush the dust and dirt into the cereal box, and his hand was beginning to hurt. But just when he was about ready to stop for the day, he saw something in the corner of the step just below the iron gate of the funeral parlor.

He leaned over to take a closer look. A tooth. A human tooth, almost covered by a fine gray powder that could have been dirt but might have been ash, Bernie wasn't sure.

He stared. Carefully he reached down and picked it up, then dropped it into his cereal box.

"Looking for something?" came a voice behind him; turning, Bernie found himself staring into the dark, searching eyes of Moe, the mortician.

Five

MAN IN A RAINCOAT

Bernie's knees shook. "Uh . . . dimes and nickels," he said. "Stuff like that."

"Well, it looks to me as though you're sweeping up—think we don't take care of the place the way we should," Moe said. "That's bad for business, you know."

Bernie stared.

"Your dad put you up to this? Getting a little tired of all the cement dust and trash and noise?"

"What?"

"You tell him we'll have the place clean and tidy for the grand opening. He doesn't need to worry," Moe said, opening the iron gate and going up the walk.

Whew, Bernie thought. And clutching the cereal box, he went around to the wall by the alley where Weasel and Georgene were waiting. He showed them the tooth.

"Wow!" said Weasel. "It's not just a kid's tooth, either. It's ragged and yellow like a grown man's."

"Two gold fillings on top and a cement filling on one side," said Georgene. "If it matches a tooth in the vice president's dental records, we can be sure the vice president is around here somewhere."

"A little bit here, a little bit there," said Weasel.

Georgene looked at Bernie. "Don't you think you ought to tell Feeney?"

"What if he thinks the whole idea is stupid and throws the tooth away?" said Bernie. "No. If the police get suspicious enough to question Moe and Joe, we'll show it to them then."

Officer Feeney was very upset. As Bernie was walking Mixed Blessing the next day, he stopped to talk to the policeman there on the corner. Everyone, it seemed, from the regulars there in the hotel to the clerks in the stores, was talking about the robbery at the Higgins Company, the blood on the carpet, and the disappearance of the vice president himself.

"Fourteen years on the force, and what do I get?" Feeney said. "Foot patrol on the looniest beat in town. If I just had a chance to work on that case, I'd solve it, I'll bet, and get myself transferred to homicide."

"You don't think the other cops can solve it?" Bernie asked, as the Great Dane sniffed at Feeney's nightstick.

28

"They don't ask the right questions," Feeney said. "Take the blood, now. Blood is found on the carpet in the vice president's office, but how do they know it was *his* blood? And even if it was, the vice president could have shot himself in the leg where it wouldn't bother him too much, just to fool the police and look like he was the victim."

That was something Bernie hadn't thought about. All the excitement he'd felt earlier about helping solve the case seemed to leak out of his chest, like air from a balloon.

"Now I'm not saying the vice president *did* shoot himself, see. Not saying that he made off with the money. He could be dead as a doornail this very second. All I'm saying is that there are questions to be asked, and if *I* was on the case, I'd be asking them."

"Would a vice president really do that? Rob his own company?" Bernie asked.

"Why, Bernie, a *president* would rob his own mother if he was that kind of man. Steal from his father and kick his own grandmother down the stairs."

"But he'd never robbed the company before, had he? Why would he do it now?"

"Of *course* he never did it before—wouldn't be vice president if he had," said Feeney. "But there's a first time for everything. He could have had this idea in the back of his head for twenty years and just now got the chance to do it."

"But the radio reported that all the employees at Higgins Roofing said what a fine, upstanding man he was," said Bernie, still unconvinced.

"Huh!" scoffed Feeney. "How *else* can a man stand, let me ask you, but up? Of *course* they all say good things about him, but that's because he's dead. Did you ever notice, Bernie, how when someone dies, everyone says what a fine man he was? You ever read that anybody said, 'He was an ornery cuss, and it's a durn good thing he's gone'? Of course not."

At dinner that evening, Bernie told his family what Officer Feeney had said.

"Feeney is full of fruitcake," said Delores. "If there was any reason to suspect the vice president himself, the other policemen would have thought of it."

"Don't speak badly of Officer Feeney, my dear," said her father. "Someday he may save your life."

"Well, if he doesn't, I don't want people going around saying they liked me if they didn't. And if I die and Steven Carmichael comes to the funeral and weeps, you can tell him that the last words from my lips were 'Steven stinks.'"

Joseph had said very little through dinner, but now he put down his fork and wiped his mouth. "You know," he said, "Feeney has a point. It *could* have been the vice president. I think I'll walk over to the Higgins Company myself and take Mixed Blessing just to let him sniff at that blood on the floor. If it *does* belong to the vice president, maybe Mixed Blessing can lead us to the body."

"Could I go, too?" Bernie begged. "Please?"

"If you are polite and respectful and speak only when spoken to, you may," said his mother.

The Higgins Company was only two blocks up the street, and three blocks over. Bernie was there with his brother and Mixed Blessing in ten minutes.

Joseph explained to the guard how he thought the Great Dane might be useful.

"Worth a try," said the guard, so he lifted the yellow tape that surrounded the scene of the crime, and Bernie and Joseph led the large dog over to the red spots on the carpet.

Mixed Blessing sniffed. He snorted and panted, then ran around three times in a circle and over to the door leading to the hallway.

"He's picked up the scent!" cried Bernie.

"Follow him!" said the guard.

Down the hall they went, Mixed Blessing and the guard, Bernie and Joseph. When they came to the staircase, down went the dog, the others behind him, and into the furnace room. And there, behind the water heater, was a chuck roast from the A & P, one corner slit open.

"See?" said Officer Feeney, when the story came out in the paper the next day.

Police Search for Vice President After Discovery of 3-lb Chuck Roast

"What did I tell you?" Feeney went on. "I had that figured out myself—all but the roast. Now the tune changes, eh? Now the worm turns. Now the wind takes a different direction, and it's a whole new kettle of fish! A brand new ballgame. A fine upstanding citizen, huh? Why, after smearing that blood around his office, the vice president could be on his way to Mexico."

"Is that where you think he is—Mexico?" Bernie asked.

Feeney looked thoughtful and tapped his nightstick against his leg. "Now that I think on it, Bernie, I don't believe he is. I figure he's hiding right here in Middleburg, waiting for his getaway."

"Why?"

"Because his car's still where he parked it. Everyone knows him, and no one at the bus station has seen him leave. I asked around. As soon as the robbery was discovered, the police sent out an all points bulletin. No sign of any robbers or the vice president either. You don't happen to have any nonregistered guests in your rooms, do you?"

"Of course not. If someone was in our rooms, we'd know."

"You've checked them all yourself?"

"Not exactly."

"Well, that's the first thing to do. What you do is you take a key and look in every one of those vacant rooms. You find a pillow that's rumpled, a towel that's been used, or a dirty bathtub, you let me know. Why, a robber, a liar, and a cheat all three could live for a week in your hotel, slipping from one room to another, and folks would never catch on."

When Bernie got back to the hotel, he got a key from Hildegarde, the cleaning woman, and—using the guest register—checked every room that was supposed to be vacant. But he found no rumpled pillows, no used towels, no dirty bathtubs. Every room was as fresh and tidy as Hildegarde had left it after the last guest had gone.

When he went downstairs to take the guest registration book back, however, Bernie saw a strange man waiting to check in. He was wearing what Bernie was sure was a fake hairpiece. He was wearing what Bernie was positive was a mustache that came on and off. He had on thick glasses that might even have had a fake nose attached, and was wearing a raincoat with bulging pockets that were full of, perhaps, the retirement money from Higgins Roofing Company. And it wasn't even raining outside.

Mrs. Magruder assigned him to room 52, and as the man wrote his name in the register—John H. Brown—Bernie noticed that the pen in his hand read, HIGGINS ROOFING COMPANY on the side.

Six

WHAT HILDEGARDE SAW

It was, as Feeney said, a brand-new ballgame. The tooth that Bernie had found near the funeral parlor turned out to be Mr. Lamkin's, for one thing. He'd been walking down the street eating an apple, he told Mother, and that old wiggly tooth of his had come right out in his hand. He'd tossed it away with the apple core. What's done was done, and what's out was out. And then, with the discovery of the blood of an A & P chuck roast, not the vice president, and the VP mysteriously missing, it was plain to Bernie, his family, and Officer Feeney that the man must have robbed the company himself.

His car was still in the parking lot outside his office, however. His clothes were still in his closet at home. He hadn't packed a suitcase, the newspaper said, or taken his checkbook, and his wife was still certain he had been kidnapped, along with the retirement money, regardless of whose blood it was on the carpet. The last she had seen her husband, she said, was Monday morning, when he had gone to work an hour early, which wasn't at all unusual.

But Bernie, Georgene, and Weasel were equally certain that the vice president was under their very noses, in room 52, at the Bessledorf. When Bernie tried to talk to his father in private, however, Mr. Magruder spoke sternly:

"Every guest in my hotel is a guest, Bernie, and the customer is always right, unless proven otherwise. If Officer Feeney or any of the other policemen has a search warrant and wants to check out his room, I shall assist them, of course. But until that time, no member of this family will disturb the man. His hair and his nose may be fake, his mustache may come off and on, but until he is proven a criminal, he will be treated with the courtesy people come to expect from the Bessledorf."

Bernie thought it over. Several things were going through his head all at once:

> 1. He could forget about Moe and Joe. Whomever they had been scattering from the roof of the funeral parlor—if indeed it was anyone at all—was undoubtedly not the vice president.
>
> 2. The man in room 52 most probably was, whether Father thought so or not.

3. If Bernie and Georgene and Weasel were ever to get their names in the *Guinness Book of World Records,* it would probably have to be for something other than the longest coast on a skateboard, because they were not doing very well at all, no matter how hard they practiced. But if they could capture the vice president of the Higgins Roofing Company with the retirement money stuffed in the pockets of his raincoat, they might make the *Guinness Book of World Records* as being the youngest ever to capture a criminal.

Officer Feeney, however, wanted to be taken off the Bessledorf beat and put on homicide almost as much as Bernie wanted to be in the *Guinness Book of World Records,* so it would be a race to catch the vice president before Feeney did, or before the man escaped them all and left town.

Georgene and Weasel sat as still as stone when Bernie told them about the man in room 52. They sat so still that Bernie could almost hear their hearts beating, above the cicadas on this hot July day in Indiana.

"It's just as Feeney said," Bernie told them. "A robber, a liar, and a cheat, right here in this hotel. Except that we know who he is."

"But Bernie, how are we going to prove he's the vice president? And how are we going to catch him after we do?" Georgene asked.

"That's the hard part," Bernie said. He showed them a photograph of the vice president from the newspaper—not too young, not too old, not too fat, not too thin, not too tall, not too short.

"Take a good look," Bernie added, "because if we can catch Mr. Brown without his disguise, we've got to know right away whether or not he's the vice president. Georgene, I want you to remove his hairpiece."

"What?" she cried.

"Maybe we could help serve in the dining room. You could spill a bowl of soup on his head. . . ."

"Scalding soup?"

"Don't worry. Our soup is never hot enough in the first place. Then Weasel could take a towel to wipe his face, removing his glasses, his nose, and his mustache. And if it *is* the vice president, I'll be right there with his picture from the newspaper and will announce to the whole dining room who he is."

"And if it's not, and he knocks us clear to China . . . ?"

"Then we'll make the *Guinness Book of World Records* for that," Bernie joked.

"I have a better idea," said Weasel. "After Georgene spills the soup on his head and lifts off his hairpiece, *you* grab a towel and remove his nose and mustache,

Bernie, and *I'll* be waiting off to one side with his photograph. Okay?"

Bernie sighed. "It was a lousy idea," he said. "But meanwhile, we've got to take shifts so that one of us is watching that man all day. We can't let him out of our sight for a minute."

He was relieved when his own mother brought the subject up at dinner. Weasel was on surveillance duty outside the hotel dining room, and Bernie was trying not to watch the way Lester was eating his spaghetti when Mrs. Magruder simply put down her water glass in the family apartment and said to her husband, "There's something strange about that man in room 52, Theodore."

"Strange, my dear? In what way?"

"Everything about him seems phony—his hair, his glasses, his mustache, his nose. . . ."

"Is he the robber?" Lester piped up from his side of the table.

"Don't talk about our guests in front of the children," said Mr. Magruder. "He might simply be an unfortunate man who lost his looks early and is trying to make up for the fact that nature neglected him."

"Nature didn't just neglect him, nature forgot him," said Delores. "He is one of the ugliest men I ever saw."

"He makes me uneasy, Theodore," Mother continued. "He could be anyone."

38

"Well, if he's Steven Carmichael come in disguise to see if I've married yet, or to say he's sorry he jilted me, I'll take both the rug he's wearing on his head and that phony nose and eyeglasses, and flush them down the toilet, followed by Carmichael himself," said Delores.

Theodore looked sternly about the table. "This kind of talk simply will not do. Not do at all. What is the motto of this hotel? Say it, each of you, loud and clear."

Dutifully the family chanted it over their meat loaf and gravy:

> *"Customers first;*
> *Employees second;*
> *Ourselves last."*

"Hildegarde," Bernie said later to the red-haired maid who had been cleaning the hotel since Mr. Magruder became the new manager. "I need to ask a special favor of you, and you've got to keep it secret."

Hildegarde's eyes opened wide and her pasty face, as pale as mashed potatoes, turned in Bernie's direction. "Oh, no you don't, Bernie Magruder. I'll not do your snooping and spying for you, no thank you indeed."

"Even if it would save your job?" Bernie asked, knowing he was really pushing it. "Even to save the hotel? Maybe even your life?"

"W—what is it?" Hildegarde asked.

"All I want to know is, when you were cleaning room 52 this morning, did you notice anything unusual?"

"I didn't clean it."

"You didn't?"

"I walked right in and out again."

"You didn't see anything unusual at all?"

"Oh, I saw plenty. I saw somebody's hair on the dresser, somebody's eyeglasses on the table, somebody's mustache on the nightstand, and somebody's nose on a chair, and I said to myself, 'Hildegarde, if you don't get out of here this minute, somebody's legs and feet is going to walk right out of that closet and get you.'"

"Mr. Brown wasn't in?"

"He was in the shower, is where, and I didn't stay around long enough to watch him put all his parts back on again."

"Thanks, Hildegarde," said Bernie. "That's all I wanted to know."

"Okay," Bernie told Georgene and Weasel later. "We know for certain he's in disguise, and I know he had a pen from the Higgins Roofing Company. What we *don't* know is what he looks like without the disguise—whether he matches the photo from the newspaper or not. We'll follow him everywhere he goes, and if we haven't found out who he is in a week, we'll do the soup-over-the-head routine."

The problem was, the man didn't go anywhere. Whenever Bernie and Georgene and Weasel were watching him, in fact, he seemed to be watching them. It made Bernie's mother very uneasy.

"He hardly even talks to us, Theodore," Bernie heard her say behind the registration desk. "I say 'Good morning,' and he only grunts. I ask if his room is satisfactory, and he only nods. I ask if he wants another cup of coffee and he shakes his head."

"Then it is obvious to me what he is after," said Father.

"What?"

"To be left alone. He came to our hotel for peace and quiet, and peace and quiet he shall have. He shall not be disturbed, annoyed, harassed, perturbed, upset, or discombobulated. I want this family to treat each customer, even the man in room 52, as though he were king of England."

"It's a queen, my dear."

"Well, if there *were* a king, treat him as though he were that man."

That made it more difficult, Bernie knew, but even kings probably had soup spilled on them accidentally.

Mr. Brown went to bed early that night, which meant he'd probably be up early the next morning, so

41

Bernie had to be ready. He went to bed early, too. Lewis, the cat, was asleep on Lester's bed below, but Clark, the other cat, had crawled up to keep Bernie company.

"Bernie," came Lester's voice from below, "if Dad ever took all our money and ran away, what would we do?"

"Lester, Dad would never do that."

"That's what the vice president's wife thought. He has kids, too. The newspaper said so."

"Well, I don't know the answer to why he ran off with the money, Lester, if he *did* rob the company, but you don't have to worry about Dad because we don't have enough money to even bother with."

"Oh," said Lester.

They lay quietly for a time.

"If we ever start getting rich, Bernie, will you tell me?"

"Why?"

"So I can start worrying."

"Go to sleep, Lester," Bernie said.

He lay for a while looking out the window. He had to admit that this very thought had crossed his mind. Sometimes when people got a lot of money it changed them. Made them think that money was going to make them happy, not the wife and children they'd always loved.

Something caught his eye outside the window and

Bernie sat straight up. A man in a baseball cap again, climbing *down* the fire escape on the funeral home. Bernie quickly threw off the sheet and jumped down off his bunk to the floor. When he reached the window, however, the man was gone.

Seven

BIRD TALK

Whatever Moe or Joe was doing on the roof of the funeral parlor at night didn't seem important anymore, as long as Bernie could keep track of the man in 52. Most of the people in Middleburg had lived there for a long time. For this reason, most people knew everyone else or, if they didn't know them by name, recognized the faces of people on the streets and in the stores.

And this is what made Bernie so sure that the man in 52 was the vice president, who knew he could not get out of town without being recognized. There was something familiar about him, though what it was, Bernie didn't know. And while there were pens all over town with HIGGINS ROOFING COMPANY on them, it did seem very odd indeed for a stranger to register at the hotel and just *happen* to have a Higgins Roofing Company pen in his pocket.

No, there could be only one answer: The vice president, having kept the retirement money in his office safe, decided to steal the funds, and make it appear that a robbery had taken place. He had purchased a chuck roast at the A & P, slit the package, and spilled the blood on the carpet, smearing it on the handle of the safe and wall. He had left his car, his clothes, his checkbook—anything that a person would ordinarily take with him—to convince the police that he himself had been kidnapped or killed. Now he was waiting, in disguise, at the Bessledorf Hotel until he could get out of town unnoticed.

The police had an officer stationed at the bus depot checking anyone who left. The nearest train station or airport was twenty-five miles away, and the vice president's picture had been faxed to every police station in Indiana. No one had seen him at all. And because the robbery had been discovered within an hour after the vice president left home and disappeared, the police felt quite sure that the man was still somewhere in Middleburg.

Bernie was relieved to see the man from room 52 in the hotel dining room the next morning, having breakfast.

"We've made a big mistake in not watching Mr. Brown twenty-four hours a day," he told Georgene and Weasel. "We were just lucky this time that he didn't take off in the middle of the night. When he leaves, it will be three o'clock in the morning, I'll bet, probably without paying his bill. One of us should be up all night watching. We could take turns."

"Not me," said Weasel. "I'd fall asleep."

"Not me," said Georgene. "I've already been grounded once this month for coming home a half hour late. If I stayed out all night, I'd probably be grounded till Christmas."

Bernie thought about it. "We don't have to worry that he'll slip out through the lobby, because Mixed Blessing barks if any of the guests tries to get out the door after Dad locks up for the night. What I worry about is that he might try to crawl out the window. Mom gave him a room on the first floor."

Bernie, Georgene, and Weasel sat sprawled on the couch in the lobby, watching Salt Water prance about on his perch.

"I've got it!" said Georgene suddenly.

"What?"

"Bells."

"Bells?"

"Mom's got this string of sleigh bells that she keeps on our front door at Christmas. When you open the door, you can hear the bells halfway down the block. We could hang them on the outside of his window."

"And if he opens his window to get some air, it's symphony time at the Bessledorf," said Weasel.

"He won't need to open his window; we're air-conditioned," said Bernie. "So it's settled. Between the dog and the bells, we'll know if he tries to get away at night, and during the day, we'll be watching him every waking minute."

While Georgene went home to get the sleigh bells, Bernie and Weasel waited for Mr. Brown to finish breakfast. And while they waited, Bernie tried to teach Salt Water to say, "Robber, liar, cheat."

"Wouldn't it be great if he would say it when Mr. Brown walks by?" Bernie said. "It would be real interesting to see his face."

"Rob-ber," Bernie said to the parrot. "Rob-ber. Robber, liar, cheat. Say it."

Salt Water watched him with one beady eye and began to walk more quickly along his perch. "Awk!" was all he said.

"Say it, Salt Water. Robber, liar, cheat," said Bernie.

"Awk! Say it!" said the parrot.

"Rob-ber. Li-ar. Cheat," said Weasel, putting his face next to the parrot.

"Cheat!" said Salt Water, and pecked at Weasel's nose.

"He did it!" said Weasel. "Say it again!"

"Say it again," said the parrot.

"Robber, liar . . ."

"Robber, liar, say it again," said Salt Water.

Georgene was back in twenty minutes.

"You couldn't find the bells?" Bernie asked her.

"They're already on his window. I counted down to

room 52 on the inside before I left, then counted down the windows on the outside. I fixed it so he'll never notice. I've got the sleigh bells tied to a long strap that's hidden behind the window frame. If he tries to raise the window, they'll ring like mad."

She peered into the hotel dining room. "He's *still* eating? Boy, he sure does eat a lot."

Just then Mrs. Buzzwell, Mr. Lamkin, and Felicity Jones came into the lobby for their daily game of cards. Mrs. Buzzwell was in her usual sour mood.

"That was the poorest excuse for breakfast I ever saw in my life," she said to the others as they sat down at the card table in one corner. "I didn't leave that waiter a tip. Not a single penny."

"Rob-ber!" said Salt Water.

Mrs. Buzzwell stared at the parrot while Bernie, Weasel, and Georgene stared at each other in horror.

"Well, I declare!" said Mrs. Buzzwell. "What nerve!"

"Don't let it upset you. Parrots are really dumb creatures and don't know at all what they're saying," Mr. Lamkin told her.

"Li-ar!" squawked Salt Water.

Now everyone stared.

"Quite the contrary," said Felicity Jones, looking disturbed. "One never knows just how much animals really know about us. It's best not to tell any stories around a parrot that you wouldn't want repeated else-where."

"Cheat! Cheat!" said Salt Water. "Awk! Awk!"

Bernie sank down farther in his chair as the three regulars looked at the parrot, then at Bernie.

Mrs. Magruder was arranging flowers on the registration desk, and came over to say good morning. "A beautiful day, isn't it?" she said as she stopped at the card table. "And how are my three favorite guests today?"

"Robber, liar, cheat!" said Salt Water.

"What!" exclaimed Mother, her cheeks turning pink.

"That, madam, is the way we were greeted this morning," Mr. Lamkin said huffily, putting on his glasses and shuffling the cards. "If *that* is how the Bessledorf feels about my patronage, I could arrange to live somewhere else. You should be ashamed."

"Oh, please don't ruffle your feathers, I mean, get upset," said Mother. "One never knows where birds pick up half of what they say. And you *know* how fond I am of you, Mr. Lamkin." She patted the old man's hand, and Mr. Lamkin smiled just a bit.

Just then Mr. Brown came out of the dining room. How could you wear a wig like that, a false nose and eyeglasses, and a mustache that was crooked, Bernie wondered, and not realize how ridiculous you looked? *Anyone* could tell that the man was a phony.

Bernie looked at Salt Water. "Say it!" he whispered under his breath. "Say it, Salt Water."

The parrot simply paced back and forth, back and forth.

"I would like to pay my bill, Mrs. Magruder," Mr. Brown said, and Mother went over to the desk.

"Certainly, Mr. Brown. Are you leaving us today, then?"

"No, I will stay another day, I believe, but I would like to pay each morning."

"That will be fine," said Mother. "Cash, check, or credit card?"

"Cash," said the man from room 52, and Bernie saw him reach into the pocket of his raincoat and pull out a roll of twenty-dollar bills.

"Did you see that?" Weasel whispered.

"He doesn't want to sign a check or use a credit card, because it would tell us who he really is," said Bernie.

Mrs. Magruder took the money and put it in her cash drawer. "Is everything satisfactory, Mr. Brown? Was your room comfortable? Did you enjoy your breakfast?"

"Yes, though the service was a bit slow at breakfast."

"I'm so sorry, sir. I only hope you will find that service in the dining room at lunch and dinner will improve. I will speak to the staff myself."

"Thank you," said Mr. Brown. He came over to the window then and stood with his hands clasped behind his back, watching the cars go up and down the street, while Bernie, Georgene, and Weasel watched *him*. Then he turned and studied Mixed Blessing on the floor in front of the entrance, and Lewis and Clark, who were asleep at opposite ends of the mantel.

When he sauntered over to Salt Water, however, and said, "Hello," the bird moved quickly away from him, down to the other end of his perch, and said in a voice that could be heard all over the lobby, "You should be ashamed!"

Eight

BELLS

"*I was never so embarrassed!*" Mrs. Magruder *said to her* husband later. "I apologized to Mr. Brown, of course, but he didn't say anything—just left the lobby and went to his room."

"Hmm," said Mr. Magruder.

"See, Dad?" Bernie said, after Mother had gone back to their apartment. "Even Salt Water knows who Mr. Brown is."

"Don't be daft," said his father. "If the man in room 52 *is* the missing vice president, you can be sure the police will catch him. If he is *not*, we will be very glad we have not made a scene. Why he is wearing what he has on is no concern of ours."

What Bernie *did* discover was that whenever Officer Feeney was around, Mr. Brown lay low. If Feeney walked by outside and Mr. Brown was sitting at the window, the man with the fake nose always turned and looked away.

If Officer Feeney came into the hotel to chat with Father at the registration desk, Mr. Brown returned to his room. If Mr. Brown was out walking and Feeney happened to come up the sidewalk, Mr. Brown crossed the street and kept to the other side.

"What do you suppose he's waiting for?" Georgene wondered.

"I think," said Bernie, "he figures that if he just lies low long enough, the police will figure that somehow the vice president got out of town without their seeing him—hitchhiked maybe—and once they turn their attention to other things, he'll slip out unnoticed and start a new life somewhere else, using a new name."

The only thing that surprised Bernie about the suspect, however, was why he didn't just stay in his room. Why take a chance on being caught? Just the opposite was true. Except for avoiding Officer Feeney, Mr. Brown strolled around the lobby, and sometimes Bernie found him walking up and down the halls on the second and third floors as well.

"I'll bet he's looking for a getaway. A fire escape or something," said Weasel finally.

"I just can't figure it," said Bernie. "When I found him up on third this afternoon, I came right out and asked, 'Are you looking for something?' and he said he guessed he got mixed up and thought he was back on the first floor. Now doesn't that sound phony to you?"

"Phony as his mustache and nose," said Georgene. It was later that afternoon, just after Mr. Lamkin had finished watching his favorite soap opera, "No Tomorrow," that Mr. Brown strolled into the lobby and sat down in the big chair beside the stairs. Bernie was brushing Mixed Blessing, who was still shedding all over the rug.

"I understand that you have lived in the Bessledorf for many years," Mr. Brown said to old Mr. Lamkin.

"Almost like home," Mr. Lamkin told him.

"That's good," said Mr. Brown.

"No it's not," said Mr. Lamkin, "because home wasn't all that great."

"Oh," said Mr. Brown. "Well, why don't you move, then?"

"Well, sir, I'd miss my waffle. The waffles and coffee here aren't too bad."

"Surely you can find waffles and coffee somewhere else."

"Yes, but then I'd miss my pillow. I sort of like the pillows they have here at the Bessledorf."

"You could always buy your own pillow."

"But then I'd miss the band they have every weekend. Even miss the animals, you know. The dog over there, for example. You get to feeling pretty safe in a hotel with a dog big as that."

"I suppose so," said Mr. Brown, and studied Mixed Blessing for a long time.

When Mr. Brown went for his afternoon walk later, Bernie and his friends weren't far behind. When the man turned around, Bernie and Georgene and Weasel were looking in a shop window, but as soon as he moved on again, so did they.

It was in the park that Mr. Brown met Felicity Jones, and tipped his hat. The children got up just close enough that they could hear.

"Enjoying the air?" he asked, sitting down on the bench next to her, while Bernie, Georgene, and Weasel played hopscotch on the sidewalk in front of them.

"Not the air," Felicity told him. "The vibrations."

"Really?" said Mr. Brown.

"They're all around us, Mister . . . er . . ."

"Brown," said the man. "John M. Brown."

Bernie glanced at Weasel and wondered if he'd noticed. In the registration book, the man had signed his name, John *H.* Brown.

"*Everything,* you know, communicates with us in some way," Felicity was telling him. "The flowers, the trees, the grass, the birds. . . ."

"Ah, yes," said Mr. Brown. "Like the parrot back at the hotel."

"Even leaves, Mr. Brown. Leaves are very good communicators," Felicity went on.

Georgene threw her stone next and hopped and

skipped her way down the squares she had drawn on the sidewalk.

"You've lived at the Bessledorf for a short time, I assume—for a woman so young," said Mr. Brown.

"Well, perhaps so," said Felicity. "One has to live *some*where, you know. My parents said I was driving them absolutely nuts, and if I would just find a place to live where I could visit them on Sundays, they would pay the rent themselves. And so I came here."

"Do you work?"

"Now and then," said Felicity. "Actually, I study the moon, Mr. Brown. I study the moon and I listen to leaves, and sometimes I just sit out in the cemetery and listen to the whispering of the spirits. It's good for the soul, to listen to spirits."

"Yes, indeed," said Mr. Brown, standing up and tipping his hat once again. "Have a pleasant . . . uh . . . communication, my dear. A pleasure, I'm sure." And he walked quickly down the sidewalk.

"He must think our hotel is a home for nut cakes," Bernie said at dinner.

"Well, frankly, he is something of a nut case himself, if you ask me," said Delores. "Did you ever see such hair? And that nose! . . ."

"He's kind to animals," said Joseph. "I saw him petting Mixed Blessing this morning. The cats seem to like him, too. Lewis was brushing up against his leg."

56

"Lewis?" said Mrs. Magruder. "That cat doesn't brush up against anyone unless it's mealtime."

"Well, Lewis was. Even Clark came over and let Mr. Brown scratch his ears."

"Well, I for one, know the man is a phony, and I intend to find out exactly who he is," Delores announced.

"You will do no such thing," said her father. "Don't you say one thing to him that is unpleasant, my girl."

"I promise I won't say anything unpleasant," Delores told him, and, wiping her fingers on her napkin, she went out into the lobby to watch the evening news. Bernie followed.

It was not long before Mr. Brown finished his dinner in the hotel dining room and came out just as Delores was turning off the set.

"Well, the world is still here, I presume?" he said. "I'm afraid I missed the news."

"Nothing happened that hasn't happened before," Delores told him. "Same old thing, which is more than you can say for some people, who are here today, gone tomorrow."

"You sound like a girl who speaks her mind," said Mr. Brown.

"When I need to," said Delores. "When I don't, I can keep a secret to Doomsday."

"You get around, do you? Own a car?"

Bernie sat without moving. Mr. Brown was trying to

find a way out of town—someone who would give him a lift and keep her mouth shut.

"A car?" said Delores. "You are asking whether a girl who works her fingers to the bone at the parachute factory owns a car? I don't even own a bicycle, Mr. Brown. Not even a pair of skates. So if you're looking for someone to show you around, you've got the wrong person. I can help you buy a parachute at a discount, but that won't get you very far."

"Well, that depends," said Mr. Brown, smiling a little.

"How about you?" Delores asked. "What's *your* game?"

"Game?"

Delores cocked her head. "Something a little . . . uh . . . different about you, wouldn't you say?"

"I couldn't say at all," the man replied. "I look at myself in the mirror every day, and I look the same to me."

"Ever try wearing your hair a little differently? Trimming the mustache?"

"Are you suggesting that I . . . ?"

Bernie's father suddenly appeared out of nowhere. "She is suggesting nothing so much as that it's refreshing to have someone . . . uh . . . unique . . . in our hotel, sir. Not so run-of-the-mill. Birds of a feather that flock together can be boring, you know. And we are honored to have you here. How may we make your stay more enjoyable?"

"I haven't quite decided yet," the man said. "But when I do, I shall let you know."

As Mrs. Magruder did the dishes later back in the apartment kitchen, she said, "I am going to put that man in my next book, *Trembling Toes*. Think about it, Bernie. A stranger comes to a hotel and everyone knows he's wearing a wig and a false nose and mustache. And everyone wonders who he can be. Could he be the fiancé of the town heiress, whom everybody thinks has been killed in a crash? Could he be the brother of the barber who was kidnapped when he was seven? No, he turns out to be the tramp who used to beg outside the five-and-dime, has inherited a fortune, and comes back to find the people who used to be kind to him, to give them each a thousand dollars. And then, one evening when the stars are out, he meets the lowly daughter of the taxi driver who used to give him half her coffee when she passed him every evening, and at a grand ball, he takes off his disguise, proposes, and they live happily ever after."

"What does it have to do with toes?"

"Toes?" asked Bernie's mother.

"*Trembling Toes*," Bernie said.

"Oh. Well, when the taxi driver's daughter finds out who he is, and . . . Well, Bernie, when you grow up and fall in love, you'll understand," Mother said.

Bernie was thinking about that later as he brushed his teeth. Somehow he hoped he wouldn't fall in love for a long, long time. If your lips quivered, your shoulders shivered, and your toes trembled, that sounded like how Bernie felt when he was sick or took a math test, either one. He could do without falling in love for a very long time.

"Bernie," Lester said when the boys were in bed. "Do we have to have tickets?"

"To what?"

"The grand opening of the drive-in funeral parlor?"

"Of course not."

"Everybody's talking about it. I thought maybe you had to have tickets. Mr. Brown came all the way here to see it."

"He told you that?"

"He said he was looking forward to it especially."

Bernie thought that over. It didn't make sense. Who would come to town just to see a drive-in funeral parlor? No, Bernie decided, that was just an excuse. This, in fact, would be a perfect time for the vice president to leave Middleburg, when everyone was gathered at the funeral parlor and he could slip out of town unnoticed.

He heard the sound of Father locking up in the lobby, Delores brushing her teeth, Mother dropping her shoes on the floor beside her bed. And then, there was another sound. Bells. It sounded like Santa's sleigh, church, and a circus, all together.

Clang! Clang! Clang! Mixed Blessing barked and Salt Water squawked. Bernie was up like a shot.

Nine

THE UNVEILING

While everyone else ran down the hall in the direction of room 52, Bernie, barefoot, ran outside, Mixed Blessing at his heels.

As he ran along the alley, he saw Officer Feeney coming from the opposite end.

"What the dickens?" Feeney was saying. "You got a new burglar alarm on your hotel, Bernie?"

"Sort of," Bernie said, his eyes glued to the row of windows on the first floor to see if he could see anyone trying to climb out.

They were right outside room 52 now. Bernie could see the window wide open, the bells dangling from the frame, but inside was John Brown in his pajamas, looking both surprised and amazed. His wig was on backwards, as though he had put it on hastily, his mustache was coming unglued at one end, and his glasses and nose were both sagging.

"What is the meaning of this?" Mr. Brown was saying to Bernie's father. "One of your cats was sitting on my windowsill making a terrible racket, and when I opened the window to shoo him away, I heard this astounding noise!"

"It looks as though someone tied bells to your window, sir," said Father.

"Indeed it does, and I'd like to catch the idiot who did," said Mr. Brown.

"I am so sorry," said Mother, clutching her robe about her. "We'll take them off at once, won't we, Theodore?"

"It's Christmas!" Lester cried gaily.

"It is not Christmas, it's incredible," said the man.

Feeney stuck his head in the window. "Officer Feeney here, sir. I believe I can take the bells off from outside."

Mr. Brown wheeled around when he heard the policeman's voice at the window and grabbed his wig in both hands, then straightened his mustache and nose.

"Oh, it's all right, don't bother. Sorry to have disturbed you, officer. No trouble at all," Mr. Brown said, and quickly turned off the light.

Feeney walked back down the alley beside Bernie. "Who the ding-dong was *that?*"

"John Brown."

"A likely story. John Doe, John Brown, John Smith
. . . all the same. What do you know about him?"

Bernie hesitated. In one way he wanted very much
to tell Feeney what he suspected. He was so certain
that John Brown was the man they were all looking for.
On the other hand, he wanted to find the vice president himself—he and Georgene and Weasel.

"He likes muffins and pays cash," Bernie offered.

"Huh!" said Feeney. "Other officers are out looking
for convicts and I'm stuck on a beat where you get
bells in the middle of the night and a man who likes
muffins. If my mother could see what's become of her
son! And she had such dreams I'd make police commissioner some day."

Well, everybody has dreams, Bernie thought.
Feeney wanted to be police commissioner and Bernie
wanted his name in the *Guinness Book of World
Records.* It was, he decided, every man for himself.

There was a body, after all, for the grand opening—
someone who had tried to shave his face with an
electric razor in the bathtub and put out his lights,
Moe said.

"Let that be a lesson to us all," Mr. Magruder said
soberly at breakfast. "Water and electricity don't mix.
Delores, don't ever let me find you trying to curl your
hair in the bathtub. Bernie and Lester, no radios near

the sink. And, Joseph, when you trim the hedge with electric clippers, make sure the grass is dry. As for you, my dear," he said, turning to Mother, "never try to run your electric mixer and wash the dishes, both at the same time."

"Theodore, my love, my sweet, if you knew anything at all about kitchen duties, you would know that running an electric mixer takes place before a meal, and doing the dishes takes place after."

"Life is full of risks," Theodore went on solemnly, so solemnly that Bernie was afraid to interrupt to ask for the jelly and so ate his toast dry. "People do things without thinking and suddenly they are no more."

"Sometimes they do stupid things *thinking*," Delores said. "At the factory we heard about a man who jumped out of a plane holding his dog, and because his arms were full, he couldn't pull the rip cord, so both of them were killed."

"Speaking of dogs," said Joseph, "we had a woman bring her poodle into emergency because she was trying to teach him to flush the toilet and he fell in."

Mr. Magruder cleared his throat. "Speaking of foolish things, we shall all attend the opening ceremony of the drive-in funeral parlor. We shall keep our faces sober, wear our Sunday best, and once it's over, shall try to forget this sorry episode in Middleburg's history, hoping that the drive-in funeral parlor will be as short-lived as summer flowers."

"Oh, Theodore, what a beautiful line!" said his wife. "I'm going to use it in my next book."

There were folding chairs set up all along the driveway of the funeral home on Saturday, more in the parking lot in back and on the lawn in front. The mayor was there to cut the ribbon, and Bernie planned to slip out at the last minute with Georgene and Weasel so they could watch the bus station and see if Mr. Brown tried to get away. But it wasn't necessary, because Mr. Brown himself was in the audience.

There was a blue ribbon across the entrance of the driveway, and cars full of mourners were lined up for at least three blocks, people waiting to see the deceased from the comfort of their automobiles.

The mayor spoke. He said that there was a first time for everything, and that a drive-in funeral parlor was a way for Middleburg to enter the modern age.

"Just because people are busier than their grandparents and great grandparents before them does not mean that we don't have the same feelings of respect and compassion," he told the crowd there in the folding chairs with BESSLEDORF FUNERAL HOME stenciled on the backs.

"Just because we eat fast food and drive in the fast lane and wash our clothes on the fast cycle does not mean that deep within our hearts, there is not a longing to hold to the traditions that made our country great. That wants to say hello to those new babies who are born, and good-bye to the old folks who are passing on. . . ."

Bernie wondered if there was going to be a drive-in nursery next to the hospital for people who wanted to say hello to all the babies born that week. The mayor droned on and on. Ladies began to fan themselves with bamboo fans on which BESSLEDORF FUNERAL HOME was printed. The people waiting in their cars in the July sun began to get restless, even though the mayor's words were being broadcast on a public-address system.

Finally the mayor stopped talking. He shook hands with Woe, Moe, and Joe, and finally took a pair of scissors and cut the ribbon stretched across the driveway. The crowd cheered, then hushed. A small red light at the side of the driveway turned green, and the first car moved forward and up the drive, while the car behind it stopped and waited its turn. When the lead car passed a certain place in the driveway, an electric eye turned on the music, and the soft strains of "Swing Low, Sweet Chariot" began to play. "Swing low, sweet chariot, comin' for to carry me home. . . ."

When the car got even with the bay window, the window lit up, the curtains parted automatically, and there lay the body of the man who had tried to shave himself in the bathtub, all done up in his Sunday suit, of course.

There was a button to press, if the observer desired, and—just as at a bank—a drawer slid open with a registry book and a pen inside. The person in the automobile signed his name so the deceased's family would know he had come by. Then the drawer closed again, the curtains shut, the light went off, the music stopped, and the first car drove away. The second car moved forward, and the procedure began all over again.

At that very moment, Bernie saw Mr. Brown get up and leave the crowd.

Now! Bernie was sure of it. Now, when half of Middleburg, including Feeney, was watching the curtain open and the light come on, the vice president of Higgins Roofing Company would go to the bus station and make his escape.

He motioned to Georgene and Weasel, and they stood up. Everyone was starting to get up now, people were moving around, going off to get in cars to join the long procession. Bernie was afraid that he would lose sight of Mr. Brown in the crowd.

"After him!" he called to Georgene.

"He's going too fast," Weasel called back. "He went around a corner."

"Hurry!" yelled Georgene.

And then Bernie could stand it no longer. "Feeney," he shouted in all the talk and confusion. "Hurry! We've got the vice president."

As people stopped talking and stared, Feeney wheeled about and came running over to them, his shiny size 13 patent leather shoes gleaming in the sun, his nightstick swinging by his side.

"Where?" he yelled.

"We think it's Mr. Brown, the man from room 52. He's probably headed for the bus station."

A few minutes later, Officer Feeney and the three children raced into the bus station, but the man wasn't there.

"We've *lost* him!" Bernie cried in disappointment. "He's the vice president, Feeney, we're sure of it. He signed in just a couple of days after the money disappeared. He pays all his bills in cash, he was wearing a raincoat with the pockets stuffed with cash, he has on a disguise, and sometimes he calls himself John H. Brown and sometimes John M. Brown. And he signed his name with a pen from the Higgins Roofing Company. It's just got to be him."

Just then Bernie saw a man outside the station, heading for the bus to Indianapolis.

"That's him!" he cried, and with Georgene and Weasel at his heels, they charged out the door in back, tackled Mr. Brown, and held him down until Feeney got there. Georgene had his wig in her hands, Weasel got the mustache, and Bernie took hold of the man's nose and glasses.

And then, Bernie fell backward, his eyes huge.

"Mr. Fairchild!" he yelped, letting the man go.

The owner of the Bessledorf Hotel, Theodore Magruder's boss, slowly got to his feet and brushed himself off.

This can't be happening! Bernie told himself. And then, aloud, "We thought . . . I thought . . . I was sure you were . . . the vice president . . . !"

Mr. Fairchild dusted off the knees of his trousers, and rubbed a scrape on the side of his hand.

"Terribly sorry, sir," said Feeney. "The children here were about to make a citizen's arrest, and seeing as how you more or less borrowed yourself a toupee, a mustache, and a nose, we took you for somebody else."

"Well, I certainly did not intend to be tackled," said Mr. Fairchild, "but I do understand, I think. I wanted to come to town incognito to see how my hotel was doing and how the Magruders were measuring up. Wanted to see if my guests were happy, and I decided to stay for the grand opening of that sideshow next door, to see if it was quite as awful as I was afraid it might be, which, I'll admit, it is."

He gave Bernie a stern look. "*However,* I did not plan on being confused with the missing vice president. I knew if you saw me, Feeney, you'd figure me for a phony right off, but I had hoped to bamboozle the Magruders. Now that I have established who I am, I trust you will let me go."

"Indeed we will," said Officer Feeney.

"But . . . but the pen you were using, with HIGGINS ROOFING COMPANY on it," said Bernie.

"The vice president and I did business together many times, and I'm not the only one around with a pen like that," Mr. Fairchild said. "Now may I *please* get on that bus and return to Indianapolis?"

"Of course you may, sir," said Officer Feeney. "Have a good trip."

"Tackled Mr. *Fairchild?*" shrieked Mrs. Magruder when Bernie told her about it later. "Are you completely out of your mind?"

Bernie explained.

"Good for Bernie!" said Delores. "If he hadn't done it, I might have tackled that man myself. No one should be allowed to go about town dressed in a nose, a mustache, and hair not even his own."

"Bernie, my lad," said his father sternly, "that man could have been anyone at all, even an inspector from the FBI, come to help solve the case."

"Could have been but wasn't," said Bernie softly. He went out to the alley by himself after dinner and sat on a garbage can feeling glum. Now the suspects were Moe and Joe again. Now the mystery of who was climbing the fire escape at night, and why, was even more puzzling than before.

Maybe they were in cahoots with the vice president. Maybe all three of them together had taken the money, and they were hiding the vice president some-where in the funeral home. Maybe they had hidden the money on top of all the coffins they had buried lately, the one sure place no one would look. No one but Bernie, Georgene, and Weasel, that is.

"Georgene," he said over the phone, "Get Weasel and come over. We've got a job to do."

Ten

MUSIC! LIGHTS! CURTAIN!

"Isn't this just a little bit wacko, Bernie?"

Georgene's bare legs stuck out before her as the three friends sat on the curb in front of the hotel. Her sneakers were untied, and the laces drooped, just like the flowers on either side of the hotel entrance.

"I can think of about a hundred million places to hide the Higgins Company retirement money that would be a lot more practical than on top of a coffin, six feet under," she told him.

"But can you think of a better place the police wouldn't look?" Bernie asked.

She and Weasel had to agree that they couldn't.

"There has been only one burial since the money was stolen," Bernie said. "I think that after the first handful of dirt was thrown over the coffin at the cemetery, and after the relatives walked away, Joe or Moe hung around long enough to drop a plastic bag filled

72

with money on top of the coffin, then threw a couple shovelfuls of dirt over it, before the grave diggers got there to finish the rest."

"A little here, a little there, and anytime they need more, they just go to the cemetery and dig it up," said Weasel. "It's possible, I suppose. Who would suspect? Who would even *ask*?"

"But, Bernie, the vice president wasn't murdered," Georgene reminded him. "At least, nobody thinks he was now. This is all a waste of time. Moe and Joe probably didn't have anything to do with it. Nobody's remains have been scattered from the roof because nobody died but an A & P roast."

"Well, here's what I'm thinking," said Bernie. "Do the police have one single clue yet? Feeney says no. Have *we* seen anything unusual? I have. Twice I've seen a man in a baseball cap climbing up or down the fire escape on the funeral parlor at night. In the couple of years we've lived in the hotel, I have looked out that same window every night, and I've never seen Moe or Joe climbing on their fire escape. So why would they do it now, and at night?"

"So you think that Moe or Joe . . ."

"What *I* think is that the vice president—who knew Moe and Joe like he knows all the businessmen in town—made a deal with them. Or maybe just one of them. He would take the retirement money out of his safe, spill some blood around from a package of chuck roast to make it look as though he had been killed, then split the money with Moe and Joe, and hide out on their roof for a week or so. Moe and Joe probably fixed a place for him up there, and took him food at night. After that they probably drove him to Chicago in the back of the hearse. He could hide out for years in Chicago. Police may have checked buses going in and out of Middleburg, and they might have checked cars leaving Middleburg for a hundred miles around, but I'll bet they never checked out a hearse."

"What about his wife and children?" asked Georgene.

"I think he just took off to start a new life without them. Took his share of the retirement money and left the rest to Moe and Joe."

"Then how can we prove anything?"

"By finding Moe and Joe's share of the money. They wouldn't put it in a bank right away, not all of it. A little at a time, maybe. After a robbery in town, the bank's going to notify the police if anyone makes a large, unusual deposit."

"So we're not looking for a man anymore, we're looking for money," said Weasel.

"Then before we go to the cemetery to dig up a coffin, I suggest we check up on the roof of the funeral parlor ourselves and see if some of the money's up there," said Georgene. "It's a lot easier."

Bernie had to agree.

"How do we get up there?" Weasel asked. "Knock on the door of the funeral parlor and say, 'Hey, Joe, mind if we check your roof to see if there's any money lying around?'"

"Georgene could tell them she threw a ball up there and wants to look," Bernie said.

"How come it's always somebody *else* you send, Bernie? Why don't you do it yourself?" asked Georgene.

"Okay, I will." Bernie got up and walked across the funeral parlor driveway just as a car was slowly pulling in. And suddenly music began to play, the lights came on in the bay window, the curtains opened, and the people in the car stopped to pay their respects to the man who had shaved his face in the bathtub. A woman leaned out the driver's side, a handkerchief to her eyes, pressed a button, and signed her name to the register when the drawer slid out, then drove away.

Bernie waited respectfully until the car moved on, then went through the big iron gate and knocked at the door. Joe answered.

"Excuse me, but I think I threw my ball onto the roof of your building," Bernie said. "Would you mind if I climbed up there to see?"

Joe shook his head. "No kids on the roof. Too dangerous. Give me a minute and I'll climb up there and take a look."

He shut the door, and Bernie went back to get the

others. "He won't let me. He said he'd go up and take a look himself."

"A lot of good that will do," Georgene said. The three walked glumly back up the driveway of the funeral parlor, and suddenly music started to play, lights came on in the window, and the curtain opened. They stared. Somehow, coming up the driveway together had set off the trigger. There was nothing to do but go up to the window and pay their respects. There in a coffin lay a small fat man, his face powder white, eyes closed, dressed in a pin-striped suit.

"What do we do now?" Bernie asked softly.

"Cry, Georgene," said Weasel. "Someone might be watching."

"But I don't even *know* him!"

"But you would if you did."

They stood there awhile, not quite knowing what to do. Finally Georgene solved it:

> *"Now I lay me down to sleep,*
> *I pray the Lord my soul to keep. . . ."*

Bernie pushed the black button on the side. There was a whining noise and out came the drawer.

Bernie Magruder, he wrote on the register.

Georgene Riley, wrote Georgene.

Weasel, wrote Weasel.

Weasel pushed the button. The drawer slid back.

76

The music died away. The light went out, and the curtain closed.

"Okay," said a voice behind them, and all three children jumped. Joe stood there in his yellow baseball cap. "I'll go up to the roof," he said, "but try not to throw anything up there again. And under no circumstances are you kids to crawl up there yourselves. Understand?"

Bernie, Georgene, and Weasel nodded.

Bernie watched while Joe went up the fire escape, hand over hand, his head tipping back slightly, just as Bernie had seen someone do at night. At the top, Joe disappeared from view. For a minute or two, Bernie could not see him, but could hear the soft thud of his feet as he walked around the flat roof.

"Nope," he called down at last, coming over to the side. "Nothing here. I even checked the gutters. It probably went on over the edge and is in the bushes on the other side."

"Thanks," said Bernie.

"What now?" asked Weasel. "Shovels? Cemetery? Dirt? Dig?"

"Not until we have a look around that roof ourselves," Bernie told him.

Eleven

DIGGING UP DIRT

The problem, of course, was when to do it.

"It has to be dark," said Bernie, "or someone will see us."

"If it's dark, we'll probably fall off the edge," said Georgene.

"Here's what we're going to do," said Bernie. "You guys crawl up the fire escape with a flashlight, and I'll be the lookout below."

"No," said Weasel. "*You* go up the fire escape with the flashlight, and *we'll* stay below as lookouts."

"Okay," said Bernie. He couldn't argue with that.

But the big problem was that they all agreed it should be done about three in the morning, when the only person out on the streets was Feeney—if he had the night shift—and even then, it would have to be after he had passed the funeral parlor on his beat.

Bernie, however, was not allowed out at night after the doors in the lobby were locked.

Weasel was not allowed out after ten o'clock, period.

And if Georgene Riley was not home by dark, she would be grounded all over again.

The only thing Bernie could think of was to have both Georgene and Weasel come for an overnight, and then—somehow—they would have to find a way to sneak out without Mixed Blessing's barking or Salt Water's squawking or Lewis and Clark's meowing or Officer Feeney noticing from the street.

"Could Weasel and Georgene come over and spend the night?" Bernie asked his mother.

"Not tonight," said Mother. "In a few days, perhaps."

"Why do they have to sleep here at all?" said Delores, who was painting her nails with plum passion polish. "Isn't it enough we've got a dog, two cats, and a parrot? Lamkin, Buzzwell, and Felicity Jones? Now we've got to add two more bodies to stumble over in the night and to eat our food and use up all the hot water?"

"Delores," said Bernie, "would you do me a favor?"

"What?" said Delores.

"Shut up," said Bernie.

He went outside. What bothered him most was that

they were losing time. If the vice president had already left Middleburg, he was getting farther and farther away. If he were still here and *waiting* to get away, he could be ready to go any minute. If Moe and Joe had some of the money stashed away on the roof, they could spend it anytime. As far as Bernie could tell, the police weren't getting anywhere. He had to do something. Anything at all was better than just waiting around.

After lunch, he called Georgene. "You can come or not; you can help or not; but I'm going to take a shovel and head for the cemetery," he told her.

"In all this heat?" asked Georgene.

"It won't get any cooler," said Bernie.

"I don't have a shovel," said Weasel, when Bernie called him next.

"We can take turns with mine," Bernie told him.

It seemed as though no one was interested in helping, but when Bernie left the house about two o'clock with the shovel, he could see Georgene and Weasel meandering down the alley.

"We'll go with you," said Georgene. "But we think it's pretty dumb to do all this work before we've even looked on the roof."

"It could be too late!" Bernie argued.

They walked across the dry crackly grass, up the hill and down the slope to where the cemetery stood.

Weasel lay down beneath a tree in the shade, propped his hands behind his head, and crossed his feet. "Okay, Bernie, I'm your lookout," he said.

"Me, too," said Georgene, finding a soft patch of grass in the deep, dark shade of a maple.

Bernie carefully removed the dead flowers from the new grave. At least the soil was still soft. He pressed the shovel down into the dirt, and began to dig.

Sweat flew. Sweat dripped. Sweat poured. Sweat cascaded down the side of Bernie's face, his back, his chest, his legs. He had hoped somehow to dig straight down and check along the top of the coffin itself, but the problem was that the dirt on all sides kept caving back in, so he knew he'd have to remove that, too.

And maybe that was why, when Officer Feeney blew his whistle at Bernie from out on the sidewalk, then came marching across the cemetery, Bernie dropped the shovel, raised his hands, and said, "Okay, shoot me."

"Just what the Sam Hill do you think you're doin', Bernie Magruder?" the officer asked, his face as red as a beefsteak.

Bernie was about to tell all. He was sick of the whole thing. He was getting absolutely nowhere in solving the case, and on this particular afternoon, the temperature was 92 degrees. He wasn't getting any help from his friends, either. He opened his mouth to tell Feeney what he suspected, when Georgene, from under the tree, said, "It was just a dare, Officer Feeney, that's all."

"Yeah," said Weasel. "He bet me he could take all the dirt out of the grave in an hour and we said he couldn't."

Feeney stared at the children. "When *I* was young," he sputtered, "we spent our summers going swimming. Fishing. Playing baseball. Eating ice cream. This is about the stupidest way to spend a summer day that I can think of, Bernie, not to mention that it's illegal. Now you put every inch of that dirt back, and every last one of those flowers, and don't you be making bets like that again or your mom and dad will hear about it."

The whole family was out of sorts that night.

"That robbery at Higgins Roofing seems to have the whole town upset," said Joseph as he took his seat at the table. "People figure that if the vice president could rob his own company, he could very well rob them. Folks have been trying to make watch dogs out of cocker spaniels, guard dogs out of poodles. We had a Chihuahua in the clinic this morning that kept sticking his head under the furniture he was so confused— a Pekingese that bit his own tail."

"Well, I've noticed a difference in our own pets as well," said Mother. "Every time someone drives up to the drive-in funeral parlor window and the music starts to play, Mixed Blessing howls, the cats lay back their ears, and Salt Water says, 'Swing Low, Sweet Chariot.'"

"You think *you've* got troubles," said Delores. "Every time the light comes on in the drive-in window, it shines on my bed and wakes me up. Why anyone wants to see a corpse at three in the morning is beyond me. I was so tired at work this morning that I sewed the straps where the grommets should be and pounded the grommets in backwards. If anyone jumped out of a plane with one of the parachutes I made today, he'd soon be lying in the drive-in window next door."

"I don't know," said Lester, who was dipping his corn on the cob in gravy and licking it off. "I like hearing 'Swing Low, Sweet Chariot' at night. It sort of grabs you after a while."

"What I'd like to do is grab Woe, Moe, and Joe around their necks if they don't make a cutoff time of midnight or something," said Delores. "If folks can't get around to seeing a body by then, it's not going anywhere. They can still come by the next day."

Bernie listened as one member of his family after another complained.

"My dear family," said Theodore finally. "I am not happy with the drive-in funeral parlor either, but we have to take the bad with the good, the chaff with the wheat, the rain along with the flowers. Remember that we enter this world naked as a jaybird with no dignity to our name, so perhaps it's a good thing we can leave in a pin-striped suit, to be admired and grieved over by our friends and relatives. What is a few lost hours of sleep compared to the proper exit into eternity? Let us remember where we lived before we came here, without a roof over our heads or a cent to our names. Change will come, and change will go, but the Magruders of Middleburg will carry on."

"Just the same," said Mother, "it's not only we who complain. Everyone seems out of sorts. Hildegarde says she hears rats in the attic, the cook says her pies keep walking away, Mrs. Buzzwell says the hotel is too hot, Mr. Lamkin claims it's too cold, and Felicity Jones says if we only knew what the animals are trying to tell us, we'd be much better off as human beings."

"If we listened to Felicity Jones for more than half a minute, we'd elect a horse for mayor and ducks for aldermen," said Delores. "If you don't get rid of that Felicity woman soon, Mother, I am going to go stark raving screaming mad."

"If that happens, my dear girl, then we shall have to send *you* away, and after that, I dare say, we just might have a little peace and quiet," said her father.

Twelve

CAT AND MOUSE

"I'm going to use that drive-in funeral parlor in my next book," Bernie's mother declared at breakfast. "I'm going to have Veronica Talbot say good-bye to her sweetheart and go off to the big city to find fame and fortune. But after she becomes successful and rich, she realizes she left true happiness behind in the small town she knew as a girl, and wants to return. She left in a Chevy but goes back in a Porsche. And when she drives through the new drive-in funeral parlor, the music begins, the lights come on, the curtains open, and there lies her beloved, dead of a broken heart."

Delores, at her end of the table, began to sob.

"That's the end of the story?" asked Bernie.

"You'll have everyone crying into their handkerchiefs, Alma," said her husband. "You'll have people returning your book to the bookstores for a refund."

"Oh," said Mother thoughtfully. Then she brightened. "I've got it! They only *thought* her beloved was dead. Actually, he was in a deep, deep coma that they had mistaken for death, but when his ears picked up the sound of his sweetheart's approaching automobile, his pulse grows stronger, his eyes open, and . . ."

"I thought she left in a Chevy and returned in a Porsche," said Joseph.

"Well . . . then let's say that her beloved somehow smells her perfume as she turns in the drive, and when he knows she is right outside the window, he sits up straight in his coffin."

"Then *she* dies of a heart attack," said Delores.

"No. Bells ring, birds sing, the couple is married, and the little town rejoices," said Mother.

Lester looked puzzled. "How could the man sit up if he's been embalmed? I thought that when your body went to the funeral parlor, they . . ."

"My dear family," said Theodore. "I am trying to enjoy my scrambled eggs. I am sure *Trembling Toes* will be a sensation, Alma, but meanwhile, please let us enjoy our food."

Bernie went out in the garden. It was only a small patch of flowers behind the hotel, but Father had planted it there so that Mrs. Verona, the cook, and Wilbur Wilkins, the handyman, and Hildegarde, the cleaning woman, could take a break from their labors and have a nice cup of tea under a tree on the grass.

It was while he was sitting there, his back against

the wall, wondering if he would ever do anything himself to become rich and famous—feeling as though he might never get his name in the *Guinness Book of World Records*—that Bernie heard Woe come out of the funeral home on the other side of the garden wall.

"I should never have listened to you," he was saying. "The first funeral home in Middleburg to have a drive-in window, and it will send me to the poorhouse. Bills for this! Bills for that! Bills for the new driveway! Better we should go without a drive-in window and keep a roof over our heads."

"Dad, don't get so upset. We'll pay for it. Moe and I have everything under control," came Joe's voice.

"Control, schmole!" the old man cried. "This isn't the grocery business! We aren't selling shoes! If nobody dies, then business is bad. When the rest of the town is happy, we are unhappy. When the town is sad, our business is good. What a way to make a living!"

"You worry too much," Joe told him. "Let Moe and me handle this."

Bernie did not move. He hardly dared to breathe. Could anything be more certain than that Moe and Joe were in on the robbery to pay for the drive-in window, and their father knew nothing about it?

If they would rob a company to get money, what else might they do? Go about murdering people to keep the corpses coming?

At that very moment the hearse came up the alley,

Moe at the wheel, and when it stopped behind the funeral home, Bernie heard Moe say, "A woman, Dad. Hospital emergency room. They say she choked on a lamb chop."

"See? What did I tell you?" Joe said to his father. "People are born, people die. It happens."

By the next afternoon, the man who had electrocuted himself in the bathtub while shaving was gone, and a woman lay in the window. Bernie and Georgene and Weasel waited until the long line of cars stopped coming and then, about dusk, walked in a row up the driveway and set off the electric eye.

The music began to play softly, the lights came on in the bay window, the curtain opened, and there lay a woman in her Sunday dress, a white lily between her fingers. There was the sculpture of a little lamb sitting in lilies at the head of her coffin, which, Bernie's mother said, was in questionable taste, considering the circumstances.

"Let that be a lesson to us all," said Theodore at dinner. "Chew your food thirty times before swallowing."

"Don't talk with your mouth full," said Mother.

"If you see anyone choking either here or in the hotel dining room," Father continued, "you should know the Heimlich maneuver." He leaped up suddenly to demonstrate how you should hold a person, bracing his hands beneath Lester's ribs. But then he got carried away and actually yanked inward with his fist. A piece of potato shot out of Lester's mouth and hit the opposite wall.

Life, Bernie was beginning to feel, was risky. There was danger everywhere—in the bathtub, at the table! He told Georgene and Weasel about it later.

"I know," said Georgene. "Mom always says you can die just as easily in your own backyard. 'Never stand under a tree in a storm.' That's her favorite line."

"Look both ways when you cross the street," said Weasel.

"Button up your overcoat," said Bernie.

"Never bite down on a thermometer," added Weasel.

"Don't stick beans up your nose," said Georgene. She sighed.

Then Bernie told them what he had overheard in the garden.

That evening, Bernie was following Lewis, who was carrying a dead mouse in his jaws, trying to persuade him to drop it, not take it inside the hotel, when Officer Feeney came along on his beat.

"Do the police have any more clues about the robbery at the Higgins Company?" Bernie asked, forgetting Lewis and the mouse.

"If the sergeant knows any more, he ain't tellin',

least of all me," said Feeney. "And if I *did* know more, I wouldn't be tellin' *you,* not after what you did to Mr. Fairchild! But I don't think they're any closer to knowing now than they were before they discovered the chuck roast. If they were smart, they'd take me off this beat, put me on homicide, and give me seven days to solve the case. I'd solve it in six, I'll wager."

"Where would you look?"

"Basements," said Feeney. "Underground. Any man who robs his own company is a rat, and rats stay underground. Stay where it's dark. Check the sewers, that's what I'd do."

Bernie tried to imagine a man who had been the vice president of a company living, even for a little while, in a sewer.

"If he'd planned to rob the company, wouldn't he have thought all this out ahead of time?" Bernie asked.

"Yes, but we know a little more than we did. Know for one thing that up until the Thursday before the robbery, the retirement money had been nice and safe in a bank. Company got wind that the bank might go under, so the president tells the vice president to drive to Fort Wayne, take the money out, put it in his safe at the office until they could decide where to put it next. So there you have it. In a few days' time, the vice president either figured this was his one big chance to take the money and start a new life for himself, or somebody *else* got wind of the money and came in to rob the vice president. Where the chuck roast comes in, we don't know, but it sure makes that vice president look suspicious. Newspaper says a clerk at the A & P remembers a man coming in in his business suit, buying a chuck roast and nothing else—no salad, no potatoes. 'Hmm,' she says. 'Sure seems strange to me. What man's going to eat a whole chuck roast, no salad, no potatoes?' Bit by bit, see, the story will come out, but I would have got it a whole lot sooner, I can tell you that."

"What if, right now, you thought you knew who the robber was and where the vice president was hiding?" Bernie asked. "Would you tell the other policemen?"

"And lose my chance to get on homicide?" said Feeney. "Indeed I wouldn't. What I'd do, see, is hold my nightstick in one hand, my gun in the other, and then I'd creep up on that robber so soft he'd think it was a breeze a-blowin'. Wouldn't go in the middle of the night, 'cause I figure that's when he'd be up and about. I'd go early in the morning, or just about dusk, and I'd march him right up Main Street, a regular parade of two! Right past the funeral parlor, the hotel, the bus station, and on over to the police station. And when they took a mug shot of him, I'd get myself in the picture, too, just to make sure they'd remember who it was that nabbed him. Yep, the chief sure goofed when he put me on foot patrol, and every day that goes by they don't find the vice president, I just laugh to myself."

Feeney went on down the sidewalk one way, and Bernie went up the other. He wondered if the policeman was right—if that's where the vice president was—in a sewer. He caught sight of Lewis up ahead, still carrying the mouse. As he watched, the cat crept along the curb until he came to the grate at the end of the block. And then, either on purpose or by accident, the cat dropped the mouse and it fell, with a splash, into the sewer below.

Thirteen

THREE HOMELESS CHILDREN

When Bernie, Georgene, and Weasel gathered the next evening at the bus station to look for stray dimes and nickels, to check all the receptacles in the gumball machines, and to offer to carry bags to taxis for a quarter apiece, Bernie told them what Officer Feeney had said about the vice president hiding in the sewer.

"Gross!" said Georgene.

"Well, I don't know, there are some awful big tunnels down there, about as tall as a man," said Bernie. "It's possible."

"But what would he be waiting for?" asked Weasel. "He could sleep by day, hitchhike by night, and be in Ohio by now. If we're just trying to get our names in the *Guinness Book of World Records,* we should try something else. Why don't we try for the new potato chip–eating record? I'll bet I could eat fifteen bags without stopping."

"It's probably been done," said Bernie.

"Fly a kite the longest? I'll bet I could keep a kite up all day."

"That's been done, too."

When Georgene and Weasel went home at last, Bernie was still thinking about sewers, and when he got up the next morning, he decided to spend the whole day investigating on his own.

He started with the manhole cover at the corner just outside the Higgins Roofing Company. He looked carefully around the edge of the cover to see if it looked as though it had been pried off lately. He walked down to the storm drain on the corner, just below the curb, and listened to see if he could hear any sounds—a cough or a sneeze, perhaps. Footsteps, even.

Then, beginning at the Higgins Company again and setting out in new directions, Bernie checked the manhole covers and storm sewers for blocks around. But he could find no sign that a man might be hiding beneath the streets, no McDonald's hamburger wrappers, no stray socks, no string or straps or snaps or buckles.

"Whatcha thinking about, Bernie?" Lester asked later as he made himself a pickled-beet-and-pineapple milk shake in Mother's blender.

"Sewers," said Bernie, and decided to skip lunch.

•   •   •

That afternoon Mr. Lamkin was waiting for his favorite soap opera in the lobby. He got tears in his eyes as always happened when he watched the program, because Monica's cousin's boyfriend's sister's mother-in-law had just run off with Peter's uncle's girlfriend's life insurance salesman.

Mrs. Buzzwell was reading the personals column in the newspaper to see if she could figure out who Harold was, as in "Harold, your wife forgives you; come home," or just what was meant by, "Linda, love is where you find it. George."

Felicity Jones, however, was having a cup of tea in the corner and reading a book on spirits, so Bernie went over and sat across from her.

Felicity seemed to know that a person was around even without looking. Felicity seemed to hear and see and feel things that nobody else could, which is why Bernie decided he needed to talk to her.

"What do you want, Bernie?" she said without looking up.

Bernie cleared his throat. "I just wanted to ask a question."

"Yes?" This time she put her book down and her large gray eyes studied him from out of her pale face.

"You know how sometimes, when the police can't solve a case, they call in a . . . ."

"Spiritualist?" Felicity said.

Bernie nodded. "I was wondering if you know any way we could find out . . . *you* could find out, maybe . . . where the vice president is, the one who disappeared with the money."

"Ah." Felicity took another sip of tea and put down her book. *Mystics in the Mist,* it said on the cover.

"Is this important to you, Bernie?"

"Yes," Bernie said. "Very."

"Then here's what you must do. You must get an object that belonged to the missing man—a sock, a shirt, a glove, a hat—preferably something that touched his body directly. Then you must sit in a room all alone with nothing but you, the object, and a lighted candle. What you must do is place the object on a table or stool, set the candle on top of it, and then you must put your face about two feet away from the flame and say:

> *'Fire and smoke, and light and flame,*
> *Listen while I speak my name.'*

"After that you must recite aloud who you are and why it is you want to find the missing person. Then you speak the words again:

> *'Fire and smoke, and light and flame,*
> *Listen while I speak his name.'*

"This time you say the name of the person who is missing. And then, without blinking—not even once—fix your eyes on the candle's flame, hold your breath, and wait to see in what direction the flame leans, or the smoke seems to go. This is the direction the person has gone."

"That's it?" asked Bernie. "It won't tell me where?"

"It will *show* you where, Bernie, if you only believe. Think carefully about the direction it sends you, and perhaps you will find your man."

"Thanks, Felicity," Bernie said. "I'll give it a try."

He went over to Georgene Riley's house. Georgene was sitting on the back steps, shelling peas for her mother.

"Georgene," he said, "Were you ever in school with the vice president's children?"

"No," said Georgene. "I didn't even know his children."

"Can you *pretend* you were in school with his children?"

"Bernie Magruder, what do you want me to do now?"

"I want you to go to his house and ask his wife if you could have something personal to remember him by."

Georgene shrieked. "I don't know the vice president! I don't know his wife or children! Why would I want something to remember him by when I don't even remember him in the first place?"

Bernie sighed. "Because Felicity Jones thinks I might be able to find out where he's hiding if I had some personal thing that belonged to him."

"You always do that, Bernie!" Georgene said, her eyes flashing. "When it's something embarrassing, you get somebody else to do it for you."

Bernie felt his face turning a little pink. He hadn't realized he did that so much, but she was probably right.

"I like you, Bernie," Georgene went on, "but sometimes you make me a little sick. Why don't *you* go to the vice president's house? Why don't *you* knock on the door and, when his wife or children answer, start to cry and tell them that you used to be a poor child, living in the street, and the vice president used to give you pennies to buy your supper, and you are so sorry he's gone that you want something to remember him by."

Bernie's ears turned red now. Georgene was really pouring it on.

All at once Georgene stopped shelling peas. "That's an absolutely wonderful idea, and I'm a marvelous actress," she said. "I'll do it. We'll *all* do it. Go get Weasel."

• • •

Three children in torn shirts and dirty socks walked up the steps to the vice president's house. All the curtains in the house were drawn. All the blinds were pulled.

Georgene Riley pressed the doorbell, while Bernie and Weasel sat on the steps and looked sad.

At first Bernie thought that no one would come at all. But at last there were footsteps from inside, and finally the door opened just a crack.

"Yes?" said a woman's voice.

Georgene began to sniffle. "Please ,ma'am," she said. "If you'd be so kind . . ."

The door opened wider. "What's the matter?" the woman asked.

Georgene wiped her eyes. "Is this where the vice president lives?" she asked.

"Yes, but he's . . ."

"I know," said Georgene. "Missing. I know you're sad, and I hate to bother you, but he was always so kind to me and my brothers—always gave us pennies so we could buy us some soup."

The woman stared.

"We heard the news," Georgene went on, as Bernie and Weasel nodded soberly, "and we can't believe a good man like that is gone. Do you think . . . do you suppose we could have something to remember him by? Something he wore, maybe?"

The woman looked from Georgene to Bernie to Weasel.

"What's she want, Mom?" asked a girl in the background.

"She says your father used to give her and her brothers pennies to buy soup, and they want something to remember him by. Something he *wore!*"

The girl looked at Georgene. Then she began to sniffle, too.

"We're still hoping he will turn up, that he's still alive and the robbers will let him go," the woman said.

"So are we," said Georgene.

Bernie had never heard so much sniffling. He swallowed. He almost felt like crying himself.

"Maybe you could give her Dad's old sneakers," the girl said. "Something he wouldn't miss if he comes back."

"Oh my goodness, not those!" said her mother.

"Those would be fine, ma'am. Anything at all," said Georgene.

Bernie tried to imagine what it would be like setting a candle in an old sneaker and putting his face two feet from the flame.

"Well, if you really want them," said the vice president's wife.

"I'd be so grateful," Georgene said, and a minute later the daughter reappeared in the doorway with her sisters and handed Georgene one pair of old sneakers.

They all stared at Georgene, still holding a Kleenex to her eyes, as she turned slowly and started down the steps between Bernie and Weasel.

"What are they going to *do* with those sneakers, Mom? Wear them?" Bernie heard one of the girls say.

"I don't know, dear. They'll probably take turns, I guess."

Fourteen

CLUES

"What we ought to do," Bernie said *when the three were* out of sight, "is slip back into the vice president's house and look through the trash cans out back. Maybe we'll find something that would give us a clue."

"I thought you just needed something to put a candle on."

"I do, but as long as we're here . . ."

They went around the corner to the alley, then backtracked to the vice president's yellow-frame house. There were two trash cans out behind the garage.

"Don't ask *us* to go through them," said Weasel.

"Okay, just keep a lookout, then," Bernie said. He dumped the contents of one trash can into the other, then started picking through the things, putting them one at a time into the empty one.

"One banana peel, two rotten oranges, a broken cup, a sardine tin, an old umbrella, a Wheaties box . . ."

"What could we possibly find that would be helpful, Bernie, that the police wouldn't already have taken?" asked Georgene.

"A travel brochure, maybe, to Hawaii. Where would a man go if he wanted to leave his wife and children and start a new life somewhere else?"

"I don't know, Bernie, but hurry up; I'm getting nervous being back here," Georgene said. "Besides, these sneakers stink."

"Old sunglasses, cracker boxes, a pizza box, medicine bottles, catalogs, magazines, lipstick . . ."

A shadow fell over the trash can and Bernie heard Weasel say, "Uh-oh." He looked up to find one of the vice president's daughters staring at him from around the corner of the garage.

"We know what you're really after," she said.

Bernie gasped.

"A neighbor just called to say that some children were going through our garbage cans, and we figured it was you—that you'd circled back again," the girl said. She had long hair like Georgene's, but she wore it straight down around her face. "Mom said to tell you to come to the back door, and she'd take care of you."

This is it, thought Bernie. They were going to call the police. Was it a crime to go through garbage cans?

Was that a kind of stealing? He had not thought of it that way at all, but what could he do? If they turned and ran, the vice president's wife would know they were phonies.

Wordlessly he and Georgene and Weasel exchanged glances and went up the walk, the vice president's daughter following behind.

The door opened, and out came the mother, carrying a paper sack.

"Here are some sandwiches and fruit," she said. "There's really no need to eat garbage. If my husband were here, I know he would want you to have some dinner, so please take it, and let's all hope he comes back to us unharmed very soon."

"Thank you," said Bernie, astonished.

"Thank you very much," said Weasel.

"From the bottom of our hearts, kind and gracious lady," said Georgene, and then they turned and headed home.

The lighting of the candle, Felicity had said, was something Bernie had to do alone in private. So Georgene and Weasel went home.

"Enjoy!" Georgene called over her shoulder as she left Bernie with the vice president's old sneakers.

Bernie tried to think where he should perform the ceremony. It was supposed to be in a room with nothing in it but a table or stool, Felicity had said—somewhere he could not be interrupted. The only place Bernie could think of was the bathroom.

When would be a good time? If he waited until after dinner, the family would be lining up to brush their teeth. Just *before* dinner, he decided.

He waited until Joseph came home from the veterinary college and took over the registration desk. He waited until Delores came home from the parachute factory and went to sit out in the backyard among the flowers. He waited until Mother had started dinner in the family apartment, Father was supervising in the hotel dining room, and Lester was in the lobby watching television with Mr. Lamkin, and then he took one of the vice president's sneakers, a candle, and a match into the bathroom and locked the door.

There was no table, of course, but there was the toilet seat, so Bernie put down the lid, set the sneaker on it, stood the candle in the sneaker, then sat very, very still on the edge of the tub while he struck the match.

He leaned forward until his face was within two feet of the candle, and recited the words Felicity had told him:

> *"Fire and smoke, and light and flame,*
> *Listen while I say my name."*

He told who he was and why he wanted to find the vice president. Then he recited the words a second time, and substituted the name of the vice president of Higgins Roofing.

The smell almost knocked him out. It was the kind of smell sneakers smelled when someone wore them without socks. The kind of smell sneakers smelled when worn by a man without socks who put them on when he went out in a boat fishing, or ran ten miles on Saturday, or worked in the garden.

Holding his breath, Bernie watched the flame. Would it lean to the right or the left, to the front or to the rear? If it leaned to the north, it probably meant the vice president was hiding out in the woods beyond the cemetery. If it leaned to the west, he was probably in the bus station. If it leaned to the south, he could be somewhere over by the courthouse, and if it leaned to the right, it meant the funeral home.

Bernie held his breath as long as he dared and did not blink once. Not a single time.

But the flame did not lean at all. Didn't even flicker. It stood straight up in the air.

Disgusted with himself, the sneaker, and with Felicity Jones, Bernie blew out the flame, stuffed the sneaker and the candle under his shirt, and was about to drop them in the trash just as Delores came upstairs to get the suntan lotion.

The next thing he knew, Delores was yelling, "Mom! Bernie's been smoking in the bathroom!"

He fled to his room and shut the door.

• • •

It was very quiet around the dinner table that evening. When the meat, the potatoes, and the gravy had all gone around and still nobody spoke, Lester said, "Who died?"

"Nobody yet," said his father. "But someone is going to."

Bernie startled.

"Who?" asked Lester, eyes wide.

"Someone who is filling his lungs with cancer-causing tar. Someone who is filling his bloodstream with nicotine. Someone who is polluting his nostrils, his throat, and the very air his family breathes, with poisons."

"*Who?*" yelped Lester.

Mother, Father, and Delores all turned in Bernie's direction.

"Bernie?" asked Joseph, wondering. "I can't believe it."

"Mother and I both smelled it with our very own noses," said Delores. "Three times I came inside to get the suntan lotion, and three times I found the door shut. The fourth time I came in, Bernie was just coming out of the bathroom, and the room smelled of smoke and matches. It's not enough that his sister has to waste her life pounding grommets in a parachute factory in the bloom of her youth, but her brother is driving her to an early grave."

"I wasn't smoking," said Bernie.

Theodore cleared his throat. "Bernie, my boy, there is one thing this family values above all else, and the word is truth. Truth in thought, word, and deed. Dare to be truthful, and the truth will set you free." He waited.

"So?" said his mother. "Were you smoking?"

"No," said Bernie.

Mother bit her lip and looked as though she were going to cry.

"Bernie," said his father again, "one of our greatest presidents dared to tell the truth. Men have gone to their deaths, been flogged and hanged, because they would not lie to save themselves. *They* knew the value of truth. *They* knew that if a man cannot give you his word, then he can give you nothing. Now, one more time: Were you or were you not smoking in our bathroom?"

"No," said Bernie. "I wasn't."

"Go to your room, Bernie. I will have no more lies at this table," said his father.

Bernie started to take his meat loaf with him, but his father said, "With*out* your dinner, if you please."

Bernie left the meat loaf. He lay for a long time on his back on the top bunk and thought about life and death and in-between. The missing vice president was certainly causing him a lot of trouble, and if he were down in a sewer hiding out, Bernie hoped he was truly miserable.

The door opened and Lester came in.

"I smuggled out a potato for you, Bernie," he said, and passed it up to Bernie in a paper napkin. It was covered with ketchup. Bernie took a small bite.

"Thanks," he said.

"If you weren't smoking, Bernie," Lester asked, "what *were* you doing in the bathroom?"

"Lighting a candle in an old sneaker," Bernie said.

"You're weird, Bernie," said Lester, and he went outside to play.

Fifteen

MONEY FROM HEAVEN

*To add to Bernie's troubles, people started finding twenty-*dollar bills the next day, but Bernie wasn't one of them.

Mrs. Verona, the cook, found one in the garden, right to the left of the pansies. Joseph found one when he went out the door to his car to leave for the veterinary college, and Lester was simply sitting out on the curb eating a bagel spread with cream cheese and pickle relish when he saw a twenty-dollar bill lying in the street with tire tracks over the face of Andrew Jackson.

"It is quite possible," Theodore told his family and staff, "that some kindly soul had the misfortune of having his money whipped from his hands by a mischievous breeze just as he was about to put it away in his wallet. I have therefore informed Officer Feeney that we, at this hotel, have found an unspecified amount of money in an unnamed sort of bill. If it is not claimed within a week, Officer Feeney assures me, the money will belong to us, but meanwhile I shall appreciate your turning in any more that you find, and I will keep it here for you in the safe behind the registration desk. Truth and honesty," he added, turning to Bernie, "is the better part of valor."

Bernie sighed. Then he went outside and kicked an empty bottle as far down the block as he could. When Felicity Jones came out to read poetry on the bench in the garden, and asked him how the candle session went, he said, "Oh, go sit on your pansies," which was about the worst thing he had said to anyone in his life.

The only thing remotely interesting that happened that day was the funeral procession of the woman who had choked on a lamb chop, and the arrival of the corpse of a man who had stepped off a ladder backwards and broken his neck.

"Let that be a lesson to us all," said Bernie's father at dinner. "Make sure of where you step. Don't go walking on thin air. Never try to climb higher than your own head, and when in doubt, hold on."

"Never lose your grip," said Mother.

"Keep on an even keel," said Father.

"The Lord giveth and the Lord taketh away. God helps those who help themselves," added Hildegarde, the cleaning woman, coming through the family kitchen on her way to the broom closet.

As the green beans went around the table, Lester asked, "Has anyone claimed my twenty-dollar bill yet?"

"No, my boy, no one has," said his father. "But don't worry. It will be yours if no one does, and I trust you will use it for something worthwhile, and not squander it on things that are here today, gone tomorrow."

Bernie wished that *he* had found a twenty-dollar bill—wished that *some*thing nice would happen. But so did Delores.

"Well, if a twenty-dollar bill ever wants to come and sit in my lap, it won't bother me a bit," she said. "I work my fingers to the bone at the parachute factory, and the only thing that ever drops on me is pigeon poop."

"Delores!" said her mother.

"It's the truth," Delores grumbled.

"Well, perhaps if no one claims Lester's money, he will use it on something that will benefit the entire family," said Theodore. And then, turning to Lester, he said, "Son, you may spend the money foolishly and recklessly on selfish, material gains, or you can be cherished and remembered by the members of your family."

"I thought I had a *choice*," said Lester glumly.

"I wonder where the money *did* come from," Bernie

wondered aloud. "Maybe it's part of the retirement money that was in the vice president's safe."

"It's possible we shall never know," said Mr. Magruder. "The money itself won't talk, and unless the police find the robber or the vice president or both, we may never know the answer."

"It's an ill wind that blows no good," said Mrs. Magruder, eating her salad.

"Blessed be the name of the Lord," said Hildegarde, on her way back out of the broom closet again, and on through the lobby to home.

That evening as the sun was setting, Bernie and his father sat on the back steps of their hotel apartment to catch the breeze. Delores was inside painting her toenails, Joseph was at the registration desk, Mother was starting the second chapter of *Trembling Toes*, and Lester was out in the alley chasing lightning bugs. For a long time there was nothing to be heard but the crickets in the garden, and the occasional honk of a horn out front.

"Dad," said Bernie finally, "may I ask you a personal question?"

"Anything at all, my boy, as long as it's the kind of question that can be answered."

Bernie thought about that a moment. "What kind of question *can't* be answered?"

"A question like, 'How many angels can dance on the head of a pin?'"

"Oh," said Bernie. He couldn't imagine himself asking a question like that in a million years. "Well, this is a question about you. Could you . . . uh . . . I mean, would you ever . . . take all the money in the hotel safe and leave your wife and children to start a new life in Ohio?"

"*Ohio!*" exclaimed Mr. Magruder, and somehow that did not comfort Bernie at all.

He tried to think what other places the vice president might have gone. "Uh . . . I mean, Hawaii, maybe."

"Ah! Ha-waii!" said Theodore, and the faraway look in his eyes made Bernie feel even worse.

Finally, when his father didn't answer, Bernie tapped his father's knee and said, "Well?"

"No, my boy, I would not. I would go *nowhere* without my dear wife and children, and I would not take any money that did not belong to me, because that would be robbery, which is a combination of lying and cheating. And truth, my son, is cousin to honesty. 'It droppeth as the gentle rain from heaven upon the place beneath. . . .'"

Suddenly he turned and faced Bernie there on the doorstep. "And now may I ask *you* a question?"

Bernie nodded.

"Why won't you tell the truth about smoking in the bathroom?"

"Because I wasn't smoking, and I would have lied if I'd said I was."

"Then would you please tell me—slowly and clearly—what it was, exactly and precisely, that you *were* doing in there, and why you were doing it?"

"Yes," said Bernie. And he told his father what Felicity Jones had told him about putting a candle on a personal possession of someone who was missing, and what he was supposed to chant.

"Son," said Theodore, "I have only one thing to say, and I do not want you to repeat it ever: Felicity Jones is sister to a jackass."

"I know," said Bernie.

There was a public viewing that night in the funeral parlor of the man who had stepped off a ladder backwards and broken his neck. The people who did not attend the viewing inside drove slowly up to the drive-in window to get a look at the recently departed and to sign the register book, proving that although they did not think quite enough of the man to put on their Sunday clothes and go inside, they did care enough to climb into their cars in their jeans and hair curlers and take a peek at him through the window.

When the viewing was over for the night and the relatives had gone home, to return again the next two nights until the deceased was buried, Bernie, Georgene, and Weasel came over and walked slowly up the funeral parlor driveway, three abreast, so that the electric eye picked them up, started the music, turned on the light, and pulled the curtain.

The three children did not press the button for the drawer to slide out because they did not know the man well enough to sign the register. He was a muscular-looking man with a broad face and blond hair. He could have been anybody's father, Bernie was thinking, and he'd be alive right now if he hadn't stepped off the ladder into thin air.

"I think I'll go home," Georgene said a little sadly, possibly remembering the vice president's daughters who were still waiting for word of their father.

"Me, too," said Weasel.

Bernie went back inside the hotel and wandered about from floor to floor—up the stairs to second and down the hall to the end, then up the stairs to third, and down the hall in the other direction.

When he came to the window at the end of the third floor hallway, Bernie stopped to look out, and suddenly he froze there in the semidarkness. For looking out the window across from him, a window on the top floor of the funeral parlor, was a man's face. It was not Joe's; it was not Moe's; it was not Woe's. The face was in shadow, so Bernie couldn't tell for sure just who it was, but it seemed a little familiar. And the only person it looked like at all that Bernie could think of was the vice president of Higgins Roofing.

Sixteen

K-I-S-S-I-N-G

Breathless, Bernie called his friends from the phone in the lobby. Mr. Lamkin had the TV on so loud that Bernie could hardly hear, but Delores was talking to a new boyfriend on the apartment telephone and Joseph was on a business call at the registration desk.

"Weasel," he said, "ask your mother if you can come over and spend the night. I just saw a face in one of the funeral parlor windows that looks, I think, like the vice president."

"My gosh!" said Weasel. "Let me ask."

There was a pause as Weasel left the phone, then returned. "I can't go till I do my half hour of trombone practice," he said. "Be over then."

Next Bernie called Georgene. "The vice president's over there, I'm sure of it!" he said. "I think he's still hiding on the roof of the funeral parlor, getting his meals from Moe and Joe, and I think it was some of

118

the retirement money that came floating down into the streets and garden."

After he hung up, Bernie's heart was beating so fast he had to lean against the wall a few minutes to control it. Finally he went back into the apartment where Delores, for a change, was all smiles.

"What's up?" he said to his sister, trying to appear natural.

"Everything is up," she told him. "The sky is up, the clouds are up, the stars are up, and I am gloriously, deliciously, delightfully, deliriously, triumphantly in love."

"With whom?" asked Bernie.

"A man named Calvin Brubridge, the most wonderful man in the world."

Bernie was glad to hear it. "Does that mean you'll be leaving soon to get married?"

"It means that to me Calvin Brubridge is the only man on earth, and for Calvin Brubridge, I am the only woman alive."

What a horrible thought! Bernie was thinking.

"It means," Delores went on dreamily, "that I hear music even when there are no violins, that I smell roses when there aren't any, and the ground feels like cotton beneath my feet."

This *was* serious.

"You and Felicity, huh?" he said.

"What does Felicity have to do with it?"

"We think she ought to be tested," said Bernie.

"I don't know or care a fig about Felicity," his sister told him, "but the next engagement announcement you see in the newspaper will be mine."

"That's wonderful," said Bernie. "That is great news, Delores. Congratulations."

Bernie walked out into the small living room of the Magruder apartment were Mother was working on *Trembling Toes*. Since there was good news in the apartment about Delores, he was sure that his mother would say it was all right that he had invited his two friends over to spend the night.

"I just heard about Delores," Bernie said.

Mother looked up from her manuscript. "Yes? *What* did you hear about your sister?"

"Delores just told me that the next engagement announcement we read in the newspaper will be hers. She's marrying Calvin Brubridge."

"That cad?" said Mother. "Over my dead body! Calvin is the most obnoxious man in Middleburg. He has broken more hearts than I can count. If Delores even thinks of marrying a cheat like Calvin, we shall lock her up till she comes to her senses."

Bernie wished he had asked his mother about Georgene and Weasel first. He imagined Delores being locked up in a room on the third floor of the hotel and peering ghostlike out the window at night, like the vice president was doing next door.

"Then we'll talk her out of it," he told his mother. "Georgene and Weasel are coming over to spend the night, remember? The three of us will talk her out of it."

"Tonight?" said Mother. "They're coming over tonight?"

"Don't you remember?" Bernie said, hoping that would do.

Mrs. Magruder looked confused. "But where will Georgene sleep?"

"She says she'll sleep on the couch in the lobby. Don't worry."

"Well, please let me know if you have any success with your sister," Mother said. "When Delores gets an idea in her head, it takes a monkey wrench to get it out."

Oh man, thought Bernie.

Georgene arrived first carrying her sleeping bag and plunked it down in one corner of the lobby. The first thing out of her mouth was, "What time are we going to climb onto the roof?"

"Later," Bernie told her. "But we've got a job to do first. We've got to convince Delores not to marry her boyfriend."

"Who is he?"

Bernie sighed. He seemed to be doing a lot of sighing lately. "Calvin Brubridge. Mom says he's a cad."

"Calvin Brubridge?" cried Georgene. "He's my aunt's boyfriend! At least, I *thought* he was!"

"Then he *is* a cad," said Bernie. "A cad and a louse. Go tell Delores."

"Oh no, you don't, Bernie. I'm not about to be eaten alive. Wait till Weasel comes. We'll think of something."

Weasel came a little later after his trombone practice, and Delores was standing at the back door of the apartment, looking up at the moon, a dreamy smile on her face. When Bernie, Georgene, and Weasel walked past her, she didn't even notice.

Georgene had worked it all out. While Bernie and Weasel stood on the flagstone patio turning a jump rope, Georgene did the jumping there in the moonlight, and as she jumped, she recited this verse:

> *"Sue and Cal-vin,*
> *By the tree.*
> *K-I-S-S-I-N-G.*
> *How many times*
> *Did Cal-vin kiss her?*
> *One . . .*
> *Two . . .*
> *Three . . .*
> *Four . . ."*

Delores blinked. "Who?" she asked.

"Who what?" said Bernie.

"Who is Georgene talking about?"

"My aunt and her boyfriend," Georgene said, not even missing a step.

"Her boyfriend?" asked Delores, looking alarmed. "What is her boyfriend's last name?"

"Brubridge," said Georgene. "Calvin Brubridge. At least she *thinks* he's her boyfriend, but he's kissed every girl in town."

"What?" cried Delores, and her voice was so loud that not only did Georgene miss a step, but Bernie and Weasel both dropped the rope.

With a wail like a fire siren, Delores rushed back inside and down the hall to her room.

"*Now* we've done it!" said Georgene. "I suppose I'll have to tell my aunt next that Calvin the Cad was sweet-talking Delores, and then *she'll* cry."

Mrs. Magruder came outside to see what was wrong, and when Bernie told her that Delores had probably broken up with Calvin, Mother got out the ice cream and said that Bernie and his friends could have as much as they liked.

Delores, however, was not to be comforted. She cried so hard and so loudly that the cats hid under the sofa. Mixed Blessing howled and Salt Water paced nervously back and forth on his perch, squawking, "Get the mop! Get the mop!"

Mr. Lamkin, Mrs. Buzzwell, and Felicity Jones appeared at the door of the apartment in their nightclothes.

"If you *please*, Mrs. Magruder, we are all trying to sleep," Mrs. Buzzwell said.

"Whatever you're doing to that poor girl, stop!" ordered Mr. Lamkin.

"It's a broken heart," Mother told them quietly.

"Oh," said Mrs. Buzzwell. "Well, the only cure for that is time."

"Try spirits of ammonia mixed with a little lemon," said Felicity.

"Nonsense," said Mr. Lamkin. "The cure to anything is something to eat. Would you mind if we joined you for ice cream, Mrs. Magruder?"

"Do sit down," said Mother. "If you can't sleep, you might as well be comfortable."

Theodore, Bernie's father, had just finished locking up in the lobby, and when he walked into the apartment, he saw eight people around the kitchen table, including Lester in his pajamas, all eating fudge ripple ice cream with sugar sprinkles on top.

"Is there something wrong with the hotel dining room?" he asked.

"We are just being neighborly, Theodore," said Mother. "That wailing you hear is not the volunteer fire department, but your very own daughter, Delores, suffering from a broken heart. No one seems able to sleep, so the least we can do is offer them nourishment."

"Alma, my dear, my sweet, you are absolutely right,"

said her husband. "Time will heal Delores, but ice cream soothes the stomach."

Delores finally quieted down about midnight. Georgene had spread out her sleeping bag on the couch in the lobby, and Bernie and Weasel, squeezed into the top bunk in Bernie's room, waited for Lester, below, to fall asleep. When at last they heard him blowing little bubbles through his lips, making a slight whistling sound, and breathing deeply, they crawled down out of the bunk bed, took the flashlight from Bernie's drawer, and went softly out into the lobby to get Georgene.

Seventeen

ON THE ROOF

The first problem was what door they should go out. The door to the lobby was locked, and only Theodore Magruder had the key. There were fire exits and back doors and side doors, of course, but if any of these were opened after eleven at night, an alarm went off at the police station.

"We've got to climb out a window," Bernie said. "Come on back to my bedroom, and we'll go out that one."

The second problem, of course, was Lester, and whether or not he would stay asleep. Everything seemed to creak once Bernie thought about it. The door to the bedroom creaked as they opened it, the floor creaked as they tiptoed across, and the window creaked when it was raised.

There was no trouble from any of the pets. Salt Water was asleep under his cage cover, Lewis and

Clark were asleep on the mantel, and Mixed Blessing didn't bark as long as it was Bernie prowling around, but stood beside them in Bernie's bedroom, ready for any adventure.

Lester suddenly gave a snort and turned over. "With jam," he said.

Bernie, Georgene, and Weasel froze. Lester began breathing deeper and more evenly again, but when Bernie opened the window another inch, Lester said, "And mayonnaise."

Bernie and Georgene and Weasel looked at each other.

"On a bagel," Lester continued in his sleep.

"Okay," Georgene told him. "One bagel coming up."

Lester began to snore.

"Stay!" Bernie whispered to Mixed Blessing, as the three crawled out the window.

One at a time, they stole across the driveway and crouched beneath the fire escape on the side of the funeral parlor. It was simply an iron ladder attached securely to the wall.

"I need one of you to stay in the bushes back by the alley, and one of you to stay in the bushes out front near the street. If anyone comes by, give a soft whistle. Okay?" Bernie said.

But the words were scarcely out of his mouth when Georgene grabbed him by the sleeve and pulled him down on the grass, Weasel beside them. They lay like the dead as Officer Feeney strolled by, hands behind his back. Just their luck. The shifts had changed and he was on night duty.

The big man in the blue uniform stopped and looked at the funeral parlor. Then he went a few feet more, stopped, and looked at the hotel. Finally he went on, humming very softly to himself.

"Okay," whispered Bernie. "It will be at least forty minutes before he comes this way again. Give me the flashlight, Weasel, I'm going up."

It was the first time Bernie had ever tried to climb the fire escape on the side of the funeral parlor. With every step, he thought about the body lying in the coffin inside, the man who had forgotten for a moment where he was, and stepped backwards off a ladder into space.

He clung tightly to the rungs ahead as he climbed, which wasn't easy to do with a flashlight in his hand. The higher he climbed, the cooler it seemed to get.

What would he do if, just as he got to the top of the ladder, he met two feet coming down? Or what if he looked down and saw Joe or Moe on the way up?

He kept on, climbing so silently that he couldn't hear the sound of his own footsteps. He had put on his darkest clothes—blue jeans, dark socks, black sneakers, dark shirt—so that nothing would show up in the darkness except his hands and face, perhaps.

As he reached the top, he could feel the breeze on

his face. Putting the flashlight down on the flat roof ahead of him, he carefully, carefully crawled over the low ledge until he was securely on the roof itself.

For a moment he did nothing but catch his breath. But gradually, as his pulse began to slow, he looked around and was glad this time for the full moon. He saw nothing unusual, just the silhouette of pipes and chimneys and vents—no form of a man coming toward him or of a man sitting.

Bernie stood up, making sure his knees weren't knocking so hard he couldn't walk, and then, turning on the flashlight, he walked softly back and forth on the roof, looking for the slightest clue.

There was an old nail, some dirty string, leaves, another ladder, lying on its side, a paper cup, dust and dirt, and a trapdoor that led, obviously, into the building below.

He could see no signs that someone had camped up here. No blankets, no hamburger wrappers—nothing to prove that someone had been living here for the past week. No twenty-dollar bills or even a ten or a five blowing about. If the vice president were staying at the funeral parlor, he must be living inside, using the trapdoor to go in and out.

But wouldn't Joe or Moe know? If the vice president and Moe and Joe were all in the robbery together, the vice president stayed on the roof during the day, perhaps, in case the police came by, and at night, when old Woe was asleep, he came down through the trap-door and slept in one of the rooms, where Bernie had seen his face at a window.

Was it possible? Bernie thought it was. Any day now, when the coast was clear and the police had stopped watching, they would probably split the retirement money three ways, Joe or Moe would drive the vice president out of town in the hearse to an airport far away, and that would be that.

What he had to do now was convince Georgene and Weasel to crawl up the fire escape with him and all three of them together go through the trapdoor, where they would confront the vice president.

"Don't fall!" Bernie told himself as he crawled back over the edge of the roof. This time he stuck the flash-light in the pocket of his jeans so that he would have both hands free. Better the flashlight should fall and break than Bernie and his head. He could imagine what Father would say if, in spite of all his warnings, Bernie should die by falling backwards off a ladder.

Slowly, step by step, Bernie came down the fire escape and ran to the bushes out by the street where Weasel was hiding. A moment later Georgene came running down the driveway from the alley.

"What did you find?" Weasel asked.

Bernie told them he hadn't seen much on the roof. "But there's a trapdoor," he said, "the kind repairmen use to get up on the roof to fix something. Every building has one. I'll bet that's where the vice president's staying and where the retirement money is hidden—somewhere inside."

"Then . . . ?"

"We've got to climb in there and look," Bernie said. "We've all got to go up there this time. I'll take the flashlight and climb in, Weasel will stay by the trapdoor to help pull me up again if I have to get out in a hurry, and you can stand over by the top of the fire escape, Georgene, and warn us if anyone starts up from below."

Bernie could hear Weasel and Georgene swallow.

"What if he has a gun?" Weasel gulped.

"Nobody thinks he has a gun. All the vice president was armed with was a chuck roast."

"What if Moe or Joe have guns? What if they're all in there counting the money when you drop in on their heads? They'll never let you go, Bernie."

"Then you'll have to go get Feeney."

"Wow, Bernie—this is serious!" Georgene said. "I wish we had the dog to protect us."

"One way or another," Bernie said, "we're going to find out something tonight. Either the vice president and his money are here on the top floor of the Bessledorf Funeral Parlor, or we're way off base. There's only one way to find out."

Georgene took a deep breath. "Okay," she said. "Let's go."

Together they walked back up the driveway toward the fire escape. But suddenly, music began to play.

"Oh no!" Bernie cried. "We forgot! We set off the electric eye!"

A light came on in the bay window of the Bessledorf Funeral Parlor, the curtains pulled back, and Bernie, Georgene, and Weasel stared in astonishment, for the man who had fallen backwards off a ladder and broken his neck was not lying down where he belonged, but standing—actually standing straight up—inside his coffin.

Eighteen

IN THE COFFIN

Georgene grabbed Weasel around the neck, and Bernie himself felt his legs almost give out from under him. It was the most terrifying sight he had ever seen. There was no more talk about going back to the roof and climbing down the trapdoor. If dead men were walking about inside the Bessledorf Funeral Parlor, Bernie wanted to be as far away as he could get.

"Get Feeney!" he gasped, and the children rushed headlong down the driveway and up the block in the direction of the bus station. They had not gone two blocks before they bumped into Officer Feeney on his way back.

"Why the dickens are you runnin' around at one in the mornin'?" he said, catching Georgene as she was about to tumble over the curb.

"Th–the funeral parlor!" gasped Bernie. "The c–coffin! There's a man standing up in the window!"

133

"You havin' nightmares, Bernie Magruder? You three kids sleepwalking or something?"

"It's true!" Weasel gasped. "The man is standing there in his coffin, Feeney! The dead guy!"

"And we think the vice president's hiding out on the top floor of the funeral parlor," Bernie went on, no longer caring whether he got his name in the *Guinness Book of World Records* or not. "I've seen a man climbing up the fire escape at night, and I think it's Moe or Joe, and we think they've got the vice president up there, because we found twenty-dollar bills floating around in our garden, and we think they're just waiting for the right time to take the vice president out of town in a hearse. If you hurry, Feeney, you might catch them all."

"I'll be ding-donged!" said Feeney, breaking into a run, and with the children behind him, they all ran down Bessledorf Street together—past the bank and the library and the courthouse and theater till they came to the bus station, then the hotel, and finally the driveway of the Bessledorf Funeral Parlor.

Everything was dark once again. The light was off, the curtain was closed, the music had stopped playing. But as soon as Feeney and the children started up the driveway again, the music began to play, a light came on, the curtain opened, and there was the body lying in the coffin, just as it had been before.

Bernie, Georgene, and Weasel stared. So did the policeman.

"This some kind of joke? Some kind of trick?" Feeney sputtered. "You think it's funny to make Feeney think he can get on homicide by finding the vice president, and then have him chasin' around for corpses that aren't where they're supposed to be?"

"But it *was!*" Georgene insisted. "It was standing straight up in the coffin. *Please*, Officer Feeney, go inside and check out the funeral parlor. We *know* something's going on in there."

Bernie knew that if either he or Weasel had said it, Feeney would have told them to go soak their heads.

But there was something about Georgene's pleading voice and the tearful, frightened look in her eyes that softened the policeman's heart, and so, waving his nightstick, he said, "I'll knock, but by gum, if you're mistaken, your parents are going to hear about this, all right. Now I want you three to come along with me. You're the ones making the complaint, you're the ones got to see things with your own eyes."

They all went to the front of the building, up the steps, and Officer Feeney knocked at the door. It seemed to be a very long time before there were footsteps inside, then a light came on, and the door opened. Old Woe stood there in his nightshirt, rubbing his eyes.

"Feeney?" he said.

Bernie felt sorry for the old man. In a few minutes he would find out that his sons were involved in the robbery of the Higgins Roofing Company in order to help pay for the new drive-in window they had talked him into installing.

"Sorry to bother you, Woe, but these kids seem to think they saw a corpse standing straight up in the coffin in your drive-in window, and what's more, they think the vice president of Higgins Roofing is hiding out upstairs."

"You been hittin' the bottle, Feeney?" Woe asked.

"I'm sober as a judge," said Feeney. "If the VP's in your building, Woe, I want to catch him before he gets away."

"Come on in," said Woe, and led the way to the mourning room where the corpse was lying.

There were actually two bodies in the mourning room—one in the window, and one in a coffin off to the side. Feeney shone his flashlight on the corpse in the window. "Lying there cool as a cucumber," he said to the children. "Both bodies behavin' themselves, if you ask me."

"Both?" said old Woe, looking around in confusion. "I thought we had only one."

And suddenly Bernie said, "Feeney! The man in the window yesterday had blond hair! The one in the window now has black!"

"What?" cried Woe.

Everyone moved closer to the coffin in the window, and suddenly the corpse rose up and leaped over the side of the coffin.

"Saint above!" yelled Feeney. "Stop! Stop in the name of the law!"

But the corpse kept on going. At that moment Joe and Moe appeared in the doorway at the far end of the room, and as the corpse started through, they grabbed him. A moment later Feeney shone the flashlight down into the face of the vice president of the Higgins Roofing Company. Bernie recognized his picture from the newspapers.

"Now what have we got here?" Feeney said, slipping the handcuffs on his prisoner.

"*This* is the vice president?" Moe asked in astonishment, standing there sleepily in his pajamas.

"In *our* building?" asked Joe.

"He was in the window—the coffin in the window?" old Woe cried, wringing his hands. "Oh, I don't think I can stand this, boys. It's bad for the heart."

"Then where's the body that was in the window?" asked Joe. Bernie looked around the room and saw it lying in another coffin. Nothing seemed to make any sense to Bernie whatsoever.

"Okay," said Feeney to the vice president. "You want to talk here or at the station?"

"Here," said the man, looking very tired. "There will be reporters and cameras at the station. I'd rather get it over with."

"Then may I say, sir, that you have the right to remain silent, to have your lawyer present, and to know that everything you say may be held against you," Feeney told him.

"It doesn't matter. It'll all come out in the wash. The money's been over in the attic of the Bessledorf Hotel, but it's in my pockets now."

"The *hotel!*" cried Bernie.

The VP nodded. "When Mr. Fairchild wanted a loan last year to put a new roof on the hotel, the bank sent our company to look the place over. That's when I noticed the attic, and the trapdoor."

"But how did you get from the roof of the funeral parlor to the hotel?"

"Simple," said the vice president. "When I was first making plans, I put a ladder on the roof of the funeral parlor. After the robbery, I hid out in the garage till dark, then climbed back on the roof where the ladder was waiting. I placed it from the roof of the funeral home to the roof of the hotel, and crawled over. Pulled the ladder over after me so no one would notice from below. Lived by day in the attic of the hotel, and at night, I'd crawl back over to the funeral parlor and check out the corpses."

"Check out corpses for *what?*" rasped Feeney.

"It was the perfect plan," the vice president said sorrowfully. "I knew everyone was looking for me. Knew that even if I got out of town with the money, there would be a countrywide search going on for the rest of my life, and that's no way to live."

"You can bet on that," said Feeney.

"So what I was going to do, see, was wait till I found a body in the funeral parlor that was about my size, then drag it out in the dead of night, go get my car, and drive off somewhere with the corpse and the money. I was going to take it out in the country, drive the car into a ditch, change clothes with the dead man, put him in the driver's seat, and set the car on fire."

"So that when the police found the car," Bernie said, "they'd think it was your remains there behind the wheel . . ."

". . . and figure the money burned up with you . . . ," said Weasel.

". . . and close the case," Georgene finished.

The vice president nodded. "Then these confounded kids came along just as I had the corpse up on his feet. After they left, I had him halfway across the room when Feeney came by, so I had to dump him quick in a coffin, and go climb in the window coffin myself. If you don't mind, I'd like to get to jail and go to bed. I haven't been sleeping so well lately."

"Well, sir, I dare say you'll be sleepin' good for the next twenty years or so," said Feeney.

"Wait just a minute!" said old Woe, and he stepped forward in his nightshirt. "What about the body? How did you figure we would close the case with a corpse still missing?"

"Well, that's the one little detail that gave me problems," the vice president said wearily. "Maybe I was hoping no one would make the connection. If the body was wearing the vice president's belt buckle and the vice president's shoes and whatever else was left after the fire, I didn't think they'd connect it with a corpse somehow."

"Sure!" said Joe. "Corpses just walk out of here all the time, huh?"

"Just, 'Good-bye, Charlie. Sorry you can't stay,'" added Moe.

"A wife wants to know what happened to her husband's body in the window, and we're going to tell her it took a hike?" said Woe.

"I would have figured it out, you can bet your boots," said Feeney. "If all of a sudden not only was a body missing, but the vice president's car as well, I'd know right off that the corpse was in the car, but it wasn't doing the driving. You may have a good mind when it comes to money, mister, but that was a plan that never got off the ground, so to speak. *In the* ground's more like it."

"Well, the people at Higgins Roofing will all get their money back," the VP said, "It's all there except for a few bills that blew away once when I was counting the money on the roof. At night I'd climb down the fire escape and go through the trash cans back of the hotel, looking for food. Took a few pies from the hotel kitchen, too. Figured to be in Puerto Rico long before this."

But Bernie was confused. "The man I saw climbing up and down the fire escape was wearing a baseball cap. I was sure it was Moe or Joe."

"Ah! That was to fool people, if anyone happened to notice me. I got a cap like Joe and Moe wear, and wore it everytime I went out at night. Figured that if folks saw a man in a baseball cap moving around, they'd think it was Moe or Joe, out on a job. Seems like *that* much I figured right."

"Well, you just come on down to the station and tell your story again," said Feeney. "Can't wait to see the other officers when they hear it was Feeney himself who brought you in. Move over, homicide, here I come!"

When Bernie, Georgene, and Weasel climbed back through the window of the bedroom, Lester sat straight up in bed and said, "Grilled cheese with sweet pickles." And then he blinked once or twice and said, "Bernie? What's going on? I dreamed I was having lunch. Is it breakfast time yet?"

"No, it's ice-cream time again, Lester. Come on out to the kitchen," Bernie told him.

They got out dishes and spoons to celebrate, and when Mother and Father appeared in the doorway to ask what in the world was going on, Bernie replied, "A celebration is going on! The vice president of Higgins Roofing has been caught, the retirement money is safe, and Officer Feeney is about to be transferred to homicide for taking him in."

"What?" cried Father. "Where was the man hiding?"

"In the attic of our hotel," said Bernie.

"What?" shrieked Mother, so loudly that Joseph and Delores appeared in the doorway, and Bernie got out more spoons, more bowls, as he told the story.

"Bernie, you could have been killed! You could have fallen backwards off the fire escape into thin air!" said his mother, when the story was out.

"I know, but I didn't," Bernie said.

"The vice president could have had a gun, my boy. He could have shot you through the heart!" said Father.

"But he didn't," said Bernie.

"The cad!" cried Delores. "To leave his wife and children and run off with the employees' money. If you ask me, half the men in town are cads, starting with Calvin Brubridge."

"Well, my dear," said Theodore, "some day you will meet a man as brave as Feeney, as intelligent as your father, as handsome as Joseph, and as resourceful as your brother Bernie."

There was a knock at the back door and Feeney walked in.

"Feeney!" said Father. "Did you get a promotion?"

The policeman slumped down in a chair and looked glumly about the room. "You know what they said? You know what the sergeant *said*? He said I'm doin' such a good job here on the Bessledorf beat that they couldn't get along without me! So the VP's in jail, the money's in the bank, and where's Feeney? Right back where he started, the looniest beat in town."

"Have some ice cream, Officer Feeney, with chocolate sauce and marshmallow topping, and you'll feel much, much better," said Mother.

"Do I get to keep my twenty dollars?" Lester asked his father.

"You do not, my boy."

"Do we get our names in the *Guinness Book of World Records?*" Weasel wondered.

"Probably not," Bernie told him.

"Can we at least get our picture in the newspaper?" Georgene wanted to know.

"That you can," said Feeney. "The reporters are on their way over right now. They'll want shots of the attic where the vice president was hiding, of the fire escape, the drive-in window, and me, of course, though a lot of good that does me now."

"Then I'm going to put on a dress," said Mother.

"I've got to comb my hair," said Delores.

Joseph even got the pets so that they could be in the photo, too.

It wasn't long before the reporters and cameramen

arrived, and soon every light was blazing in the Bessledorf. Mr. Lamkin, Mrs. Buzzwell, and Felicity Jones gathered in the hallway in their nightclothes and were invited for ice cream, too.

"It's just like I said, Bernie," Officer Feeney told him. "A robber, a liar, and a cheat could be in any room here at the Bessledorf, and you wouldn't even know it. I might not notice myself. But when a *corpse* goes walkin', that's another story."